# Mostly Ghostly 2

## Have You Met My Ghoulfriend?

## Experience all the chills of the Mostly Ghostly series!

### AND COMING SOON:

Mostly Ghostly

Have You Met My Ghoulfriend?

2

# R.L. STINE

**DELACORTE PRESS**
A PARACHUTE PRESS BOOK

Published by
Delacorte Press
an imprint of
Random House Children's Books
a division of Random House, Inc.
New York

A Parachute Press Book

Visit us on the Web! www.randomhouse.com/kids
Educators and librarians, for a variety of teaching tools, visit us at
www.randomhouse.com/teachers

Library of Congress Cataloging-in-Publication Data
Stine, R.L.
Have you met my ghoulfriend? / R.L. Stine.
p. cm.—(Mostly ghostly)
Summary: Phears, an evil ghost, wants eleven-year-old Max to help
him capture the ghosts of two children whose parents once trapped
him, and he sends a Berserker Ghoul to possess Max and convince
him to obey.
ISBN 0-385-74664-4 (hardcover)—ISBN 0-385-90914-4 (lib. bdg.)
[1. Ghosts—Fiction. 2. Ghouls and ogres—Fiction. 3. Demoniac
possession—Fiction. 4. Schools—Fiction.]   I. Title.   II. Series.
PZ7.S86037Hav    2004
[Fic]—dc22
2003026134

Printed in the United States of America

August 2004

10 9 8

BVG

For George and Marian Kirby

# i

Dear Diary,

Hi, it's me, Max Doyle. My teacher, Ms. McDonald, is making us all keep journals this year, so that's why I'm writing this.

Ms. McDonald says we should write about what happens to us every day. We should take our time and be thoughtful. And we should be honest and write down our real feelings about what we did that day.

So here's my problem.

If I write down what's really happening

to me, no one will believe it. If I tell the truth, Ms. McDonald will say I'm writing fiction, and she'll give me an F on my journal.

How embarrassing would that be? To flunk your life!

But how can I write the truth? Let's say I start out on page one here, and I write that two ghosts are haunting me.

Will Ms. McDonald buy that? I don't think so.

I would already flunk on page one.

Be sure to give details, Ms. McDonald said. Okay. Here are some details.

The two ghosts are named Nicky and

Tara Roland. Nicky is my age, eleven, and Tara is nine. They say that I'm living in their house. They keep appearing and disappearing all the time. They don't seem to be able to control when they're here and when they're not.

At first I was terrified of them. I mean, who wants ghosts haunting you in your room? But now I feel a little sorry for them. They don't remember how they died. And they don't know where their parents are. Are their parents dead too? They don't know.

It's very sad, right? I tried to tell Mom and Dad about Nicky and Tara. But they didn't believe me. Mom said I'm too old to have invisible friends. And Dad keeps threatening to send me to the Plover School. It's a really tough boarding school where you have to wear uniforms and march around in the sun all day till you puke. Dad went there, and he says it will make a man of me and make me forget my stupid ghost stories.

My older brother, Colin, was no help either. He laughed at me and gave me a few punches in the stomach that made me walk on all fours for a few hours.

Colin doesn't know his own strength. Well, actually, he does. He thinks he's perfect, and he thinks I'm a total geek because I'm not perfect like him.

You see, the problem is, I'm the only one in my family who can see or hear the two ghosts.

Why is that? Beats me.

Nicky and Tara want me to help them. They're desperate to find their parents. Here's the deal: They say if I help them find their parents, they'll help make me braver and cooler. They'll help me impress my dad so he won't send me to the Plover School.

I don't really want to make a deal with ghosts. I wish they would go haunt some-one else. But what can I do?

You see why I can't write any of this, Diary? I don't want Ms. McDonald to think I made up a bunch of crazy stuff to put in this journal. And I don't want to get an F.

So I can't be honest or thoughtful. And I can't write my true feelings in here. And I _totally_ can't write what's happening to me. Sorry.

I have to tear this page out and start all over.

Dear Diary,

I woke up this morning and looked out the window. I saw that it was a beautiful November day. It made me kind of happy to see the ground all shiny with frost. But since it was a school day, I couldn't look out the window for very long.

At breakfast, my brother, Colin, shoved a poached egg down the back of my sweatshirt. Then he slapped my back really hard to make sure the egg oozed right down to my waist. Sweet guy, huh?

I changed my sweatshirt but I didn't have time to shower. So I smelled kind of eggy all day, and a few people held their noses when I walked by and asked, "What's that smell?"

I did a bunch of interesting stuff at school, and some crazy things happened to me, which I don't want to go into.

After school, I came home and walked my dog, Buster. And then I started writing in this journal, and that's all that happened so far.

More tomorrow.

Max

# 2

**HERE'S WHAT REALLY HAPPENED** this morning. . . .

The waking-up-and-looking-out-the-window part was true. And the thing about Jerk Face Colin putting an egg down my back was true too. Colin is big and strong and very fast. That means when Mom turns her back, he can do a lot of damage.

If I complain to Mom and tell on Colin, that just makes me a whiny baby who has to be sent to the Plover School to toughen up. So I kept my mouth shut, changed my sweatshirt, and hurried off to Jefferson Elementary School smelling like a stale Egg McMuffin.

But here's the part I left out of my journal. When I ran up to my room to change my sweatshirt, I heard a cat meowing. The meowing was very nearby. Like in my room.

This was kinda creepy because we don't have a cat.

Mom is allergic. I mean, really allergic. If a cat comes anywhere near her, Mom's head turns bright red and swells up like a Thanksgiving Parade balloon. No joke.

I pulled down the sleeves of my FRODO LIVES! sweatshirt and listened. I heard a long howl, close and very sad. "Cat? Where are you?" I called.

I dropped to my knees and searched under the bed. I pulled open the closet door and searched in all the clothes I had dumped on the floor.

No. No cat.

But again I heard a long, mournful howl.

And then a chill tightened the back of my neck. *Is there such a thing as a ghost cat?*

You see, I can't stop thinking about ghosts.

I had to get out of my room. I grabbed my jacket and flung my backpack over my shoulder and ran out of the house.

My shoes crunched over the frosty ground as I jogged toward school. I didn't see any other kids. I knew I was going to be late.

I stopped at the corner as Mrs. Murray, one of our neighbors, zoomed past in her car. I waved, but I don't think she saw me.

I wondered if my best friend, Aaron, would be in school today. Monday is phys ed day, and Aaron usually manages to be sick on phys ed day. He's not a weakling or anything. He just hates to run or jump or do anything that might make him sweat.

Okay. Aaron is a little weird. But that doesn't mean he isn't a great best friend.

I turned the corner, jogging hard, and the school came into view. It's an old-fashioned-looking three-story brick building with a big playground and a soccer field behind it. A few years ago, a movie company came and used our school in their movie because they said it looked like a typical school.

Aaron and I got really psyched. Because someone said that Jennifer Garner was in the movie, and we were really into *Alias* big-time. We hung around watching them film for days. A couple of times, they had to send security guards to chase us away. But we never saw Jennifer Garner or anyone else who looked like a movie star. Bummer.

The flag on the flagpole in front of school was flapping really hard. It was a breezy, cool day. I crossed the street and began to run across the front lawn.

I stopped when I heard the buzzing sound.

It was so close and loud, at first I thought it was guys doing roadwork. I glanced around. No construction crew in sight. I felt a rush of wind in my face—and then I saw the wasp.

A large black and yellow wasp with a sharp brown stinger. It circled me rapidly, wings buzzing like crazy. I swung my arm and tried to bat it away.

It darted high, dodging my hand. Then, buzzing like a buzz saw, it dove at me.

"Ow—hey!"

It flew into my forehead. Darted up again. And then started circling me—so close I could feel the wind off its wings.

What's up with this? I wondered. Isn't November a little late in the year for wasps? Did this wasp forget to die?

I swiped at it again. And again.

The wasp shot out of reach, then dove for me again, hitting the front of my jacket, then buzzing away.

"Go away!" I shouted. I covered my face with my backpack as the wasp soared high, then hit the top of my head hard and shot back up.

Why was it attacking me like this? Was it some kind of killer wasp?

I'm not afraid of bees or wasps—*as long as they stay away from me!*

But I suddenly realized my heart was fluttering as fast as the wasp's wings. I dodged and ducked and tried to swat the thing away. A big SUV rumbled past. The driver probably wondered why I was doing such a crazy dance.

"Go away. *Go away!*" I shouted, swinging my backpack at the buzzing insect.

Swooping away, the wasp rose high, then dropped fast—and landed on my nose. Its furry legs prickled my skin.

*Don't sting me!*

I gave my nose a hard slap. Pain shot over my face and my eyes watered.

Did I hit the wasp?

No. I heard the buzzing again. I tried to search for it, but my vision was still blurred.

"Ohhhh." I uttered a low moan as I felt something tickle the outside of my ear.

And then I felt the sticky, prickly wasp body climb inside. Into my ear. The buzzing became a roar. It clogged my ear. I couldn't hear anything else.

"No—please—!"

A wasp in my ear! Inside my head! The insect had crawled *inside my head*.

I dropped to my knees. I shook my head frantically. I shook my whole body.

But the wasp had burrowed deep into my ear canal.

Please don't sting me! Please!

I could feel it in there, stuffed tightly, pushing deeper, deeper . . . vibrating my ear, making my whole head buzz. I shut my eyes. I let out a hoarse scream of panic.

And as I twisted and shuddered and shook, the buzzing stopped.

Silence.

And then I heard a low whispered voice: *"I'll sting you, Max. I'll sting you!"*

# 3

**"I'LL STING YOU, MAX**—*if you don't help me.*"

The raspy voice inside my ear made my whole head rattle and vibrate. I grabbed the sides of my face, trying to keep my head from exploding.

The furry wasp scratched me as it pushed deeper inside my ear. And the whispered voice made my whole body shudder in terror.

I knew who it was. I didn't have to think about it.

Phears!

Phears, the evil ghost. He had tortured me before!

Phears! Even his name made my teeth chatter and sent chills down my back.

He called himself the Animal Traveler. And he always appeared inside some kind of animal or insect.

I thought I'd gotten rid of him for good last Halloween. But here he was, inside my ear—stinger poised, ready to dig deep and send pain shooting through my brain.

What did he want from me?

I knew the answer to that question. He was desperate to capture Nicky and Tara. Why did he want them? Why was he so eager to get them?

I didn't have a clue.

"Max, you know what I want," he whispered. His croaky voice rattled from deep inside my ear.

"Please . . . don't sting me," I begged. I was shaking so hard, I could barely talk. My ear throbbed with pain. What if the wasp got stuck in there? What if it couldn't get out?

"You know I want those two Roland kids," Phears said. "I haven't had much luck rounding them up. They go invisible every time I come near."

"Please . . . ," I whispered. "Could you back out of m-my ear? I . . . I know it's odd. But I have a thing about wasps in my ears."

*"Shut up, fool!"*

His scream sent pain shooting through my brain. My head vibrated hard. Again, I shut my eyes tight, trying to fight the dizziness.

"Nicky and Tara trust you, Max," Phears continued, whispering again. "They'll follow you anywhere, won't they?"

"I . . . I don't know," I said, blinking hard, still dizzy.

"Guess what, Max. You're going to bring them to me. You're going to lead them right to me. You're working for *me* now, Max."

15

"*No—!*" I protested. "No way!"

The pain started slowly, just a pinch at first. Then the pinch became a stab. And the pain washed over me like a *thousand* stab wounds.

I opened my mouth in a long howl as I realized the wasp had stung me. I shut my eyes tight and pressed my hands against my head as wave after wave of pain rolled over me. It felt as if my *brain* was on fire!

The wasp flew out of my ear and fluttered above my head. I raised my hand to my ear—but quickly pulled it away. The pain was too sharp. I couldn't swallow. I couldn't breathe. I couldn't hear. Carefully, I raised my hand to my ear again and realized it was swelling, swelling fast, tingling and throbbing with pain.

On my knees in the damp grass, I held my swelling ear—and stared at the wasp as it started to grow. As big as a squirrel . . . and then as big as Buster, my dog. The wasp made gross squeaking and groaning sounds as it expanded, giant wings raised behind its swollen body.

And then with a loud *pop*, the wasp exploded. Wings and body parts and spindly legs flew in all directions. And Phears floated in front of me.

Tall and dark, covered in a long gray cloak, his face hidden behind wisps of black fog, only his empty white eyes showed through the mist. He floated close.

"You seem to have hurt your ear," he said. "Poor boy."

"Luckily, I have two of them," I said, trying to sound brave. But my voice came out high and trembling.

"I had to show you who is boss," he said, the mist swirling around him now, hiding even his eyes from view.

"You're not my boss," I whispered. "I know you can hurt me. But I won't work for you. Nicky and Tara are my friends."

He laughed, an ugly tinkling laugh that sounded like glass shattering. "I see I'm going to have to *break* you, Max," he boomed. "Maybe *I'm* your friend. Maybe you'll be in so much trouble real soon, you'll need *me* to be your friend."

A car turned the corner, its headlights on. They washed over Phears, cutting through his blanket of fog.

I saw him flinch and cover his face with his cloak. And I remembered that he was afraid of light. He appeared to shrink until he was half his full height.

The car sped past. He lowered his cloak. "I'll be back soon, Max, and I'm bringing a friend to convince you to help me."

"A f-friend?" I stammered.

"A Berserker Ghoul," he rasped. "Have you ever met a Berserker Ghoul?"

"No," I said. "Most of my friends are human."

My ear throbbed with pain. I touched it carefully. "Owww!" It had swelled to the size of a softball.

"Well, I think my ghoul friend will convince you to cooperate," Phears said. "I think he will become very close to you. *Very* close."

I didn't know what he was talking about. But I didn't like the sound of it.

"Take care of that ear, Max," Phears whispered. "It looks very nasty."

Phears faded into the fog that swirled around him. I saw a chipmunk scampering toward us. The fog swept over the little creature and disappeared inside it.

Phears, the Animal Traveler. Inside a chipmunk now.

I watched the chipmunk run away. Then, still trembling, I picked up my backpack and started walking slowly to school on shaky legs. No hurry. I was already late. And what excuse could I give Ms. McDonald?

I heard a sound. "Nicky? Tara? Are you here?" I glanced around. "Were you here the whole time? We need to talk."

No. Not them. Just the flag high on the flagpole, flapping in the wind.

Where were they? They were always appearing and disappearing. They never seemed to be around when I needed them. And I really needed them now, with Phears sending one of his friends to "break" me.

Yikes!

I felt my ear again. Pain shot through my head. My ear had swelled even bigger. It hurt so much, I couldn't even touch it.

Hope no one notices, I thought.

I pulled open the front door and stepped inside. The hall was empty. The other kids were all in their classrooms.

I headed up the stairs to Ms. McDonald's class on the second floor. I suddenly thought about the journal she was making us keep. How would I write in the journal about my morning?

If I wrote the truth, I knew what Ms. McDonald would do. She would call in my parents for a conference. She'd tell them I had serious mental problems. She'd tell them I was imagining all kinds of frightening things.

And then I knew what Dad would do. Buy me a one-way ticket to the Plover School.

I crept into the classroom. My ear throbbed. I staggered from dizziness. I just wanted to sneak over to my seat in the back row and hide.

But I saw Traci Wayne turn around. She stared at me for a moment. Then her eyes went wide and her mouth dropped open. She pointed at me and let out a long, shrill scream of horror.

# 4

**I DROPPED MY BACKPACK** and stumbled backward into the wall. I heard loud gasps as everyone turned to see where Traci was pointing.

"Sorry I screamed," Traci said to Ms. McDonald. "I . . . I thought it was some kind of creature."

Ms. McDonald frowned at me. "Max, please remove that huge bubblegum bubble from the side of your head. It isn't funny."

"It's not bubblegum," I said. "It's my ear."

Ms. McDonald put down the chalk and started walking toward me. "Max, why is your ear the size of a soccer ball?"

Because a terrifying ghost inside a wasp flew deep into my ear and stung me?

"A . . . a wasp stung me," I said. I felt my ear. A stab of pain ran through my whole body. My knees buckled. I nearly collapsed to the floor. The ear was nearly as big as my head!

No wonder Traci Wayne screamed. No wonder she thought I was a monster.

Ms. McDonald came close and lowered her head to examine my ear. She raised her hand to touch it but changed her mind. "You'd better see the nurse," she said, pushing me toward the door. "That's the ugliest thing I've ever seen in my life."

"Thanks," I muttered. Just what you want to hear your teacher say to you, right?

I slunk down the hall to the nurse's office. After Mrs. Wilpon, the nurse, got through gasping and gagging, she put an ice bag on it. I sat there with the ice bag for the rest of the morning. After that, the ear shrank down to the size of a lemon. Not bad.

I thanked Mrs. Wilpon and headed back to class. I thought the worst part of my day was over.

Was I wrong!

# 5

**I RAN INTO TRACI WAYNE** in the lunchroom. Traci is blond and pretty, with olive-colored eyes and a great smile. She's very nice but she doesn't talk to me often. You see, I'm definitely not in her crowd.

She hangs with the cool crowd. And I'm in the crowd known as "Do *you* go to this school?"

I'm sure Traci thinks of me as a different species. You know. Like a zoo animal you want to stare at for a while but you don't want to get too close to. Because you might catch germs or something.

I don't know if I'm in love with Traci or have a crush on her or what. But every time I see her, my cheeks turn bright red, I have trouble breathing, and my tongue twists up like a knot in my mouth.

Traci wore a red T-shirt and a short plaid pleated skirt over red tights. A salad and a bowl of noodle soup sat on the lunch tray she was holding.

"Hi," I said, feeling my cheeks start to glow.

"Max, no offense. But please go away," Traci said. "You'll spoil my lunch."

"But, Traci—"

"I can't stop thinking about your ear," she said, making a disgusted face. "I kept gagging all through Spanish class."

"Thanks for caring," I muttered.

"It was totally gross," she continued, gazing over my shoulder to the table where all the cool kids sit. "Like a totally disgusting horror movie."

"Tell me about it," I said. I didn't know what else to say.

"Please tell me it wasn't real. Was it one of your magic tricks?"

Traci helped me out when I did my magic act for the whole school last Halloween. Unfortunately, that evil ghost Phears burst onstage inside a giant cockroach. He terrified everyone and sent them all running out of the auditorium. Traci was horrified by the whole thing. But somehow I convinced her it was all a trick of mine.

"It wasn't a magic trick this time. I was stung by a wasp," I said.

"Well, you really made me sick," Traci said. She started toward the table. "I'll probably have nightmares for weeks."

I chased after her. "Does this mean you're not coming to my birthday party?"

She narrowed her eyes at me. "Birthday party? When is your birthday?"

"Next April," I said. "Six months from now. I was only checking. Think you'll come?"

She tossed back her blond hair and laughed.

"Was that a yes or a no?" I called.

But she was already sitting at the table, talking to her friends.

Oh, wow. Bad news for me.

What could I do to change her mind?

More horror to come, friends. I completely forgot it was phys ed day. I skulked into the gym, changed into my gym shorts, and looked for Aaron. But of course he was absent, lucky guy.

The rest of the class was there, including Traci. I could see her pointing at my swollen ear and telling other kids about it. And then I turned and let out an unhappy groan.

The climbing rope.

Oh no. Today was the rope-climbing test.

I staggered back, my heart leaping into my throat. I *hate* the climbing rope. The last time I tried it, I got rope burns all over my body.

I knew I needed to pass the rope-climbing test to pass phys ed. I get all As in everything else. In fact, the kids in my class gave me the nickname Brainimon because I'm so smart.

But my phys ed grade is the only grade my dad cares about. Flunk phys ed and I can say,

Goodbye, Jefferson Elementary—and Hello, Plover School.

How could I climb today? I was still shaky from meeting Phears. And I was afraid my big ear might weigh me down. So I ran over to talk to Coach Freeley before the testing began.

Coach Freeley is built like a tank. He's very short and very wide, with bulging muscles everywhere you can have muscles. He has a broad chest that stretches his T-shirts tight over his perfect abs. He's young and the girls all think he's really cute—I guess because of that big chest and all the muscles, and because of his wavy black hair and white-toothed smile.

He doesn't smile at me much. He tries to help me sometimes. But he knows when it comes to sports, I'm totally lame.

I ran up to him as he was about to blow his whistle to get everyone quiet. "Coach, I can't climb today," I said breathlessly.

He narrowed his dark eyes at me. "What's your problem?"

"Bad ear," I said. "I was stung by a wasp." I turned and showed it to him. It was still the size of a lemon.

"Yuck. That's disgusting," he said. "Can't you cover it up or something?"

"It really hurts," I said. "I'd better not climb today."

He shrugged his big shoulders. "No problem, Max. You can make it up any time you feel like it."

Any time I feel like it? You mean like, *never*?

I thanked him and trotted off to the bleachers at the side of the gym. I was so happy, I wanted to leap up and pump my fists in the air. I don't have to climb today!

But as I sat down on the bottom bleacher seat, I heard a voice next to me. "Whoa, Max—what are you doing?"

I let out a startled cry as Nicky and Tara appeared at my sides.

"Get up, Max. You've got to do your climbing test," Nicky said. He pulled me to my feet.

"Let go," I snapped. "I'm not climbing today. Coach said I don't have to."

"But *we* say you *do* have to," Tara said, moving behind me and pushing me toward the other kids.

"Where have you been?" I asked.

"We don't know," Nicky said. "Sometimes we just disappear. We can't control it."

"We're new at this ghost thing, remember?" Tara said.

Coach Freeley blew his whistle. Kids stopped talking and fooling around and began lining up in front of the climbing rope. The gym grew quiet except for the scrape of sneakers on the hardwood floor.

"I have to talk to you two," I whispered.

"Phears stopped me this morning. He wants me to take you to him. If I don't, he says he's going to bring a friend—some kind of ghoul—to *break* me."

"Don't worry," Tara said, squeezing my hand. "We'll protect you."

Nicky's mouth dropped open. He stared at his sister. "Protect him? How?"

"No time for that now," Tara said, pushing me toward the line of kids. "Now Max has to climb the rope."

"You can't make me," I said, trying to get away from them.

"Don't you want to impress Traci?" Tara asked.

"Don't you want to impress your dad?" Nicky added. "You have to climb the rope to get an A."

"But I *can't* climb the rope!" I whined.

"Hel-*lo*. Of course you can," Nicky said. "With our help."

"We'll get you up there. No problem," Tara said. "Hey, isn't that what we promised you? Didn't we promise to help make you brave and impress your dad, and keep you from that awful boarding school?"

"Come on. Get over there," Nicky said, helping Tara shove me forward.

"Are there any volunteers to go first?" Coach Freeley called. "Who wants to climb first?"

Tara grabbed my arm and shot it up into the air. Then she waved it frantically.

"Max?" Coach Freeley couldn't hide his surprise.

Everyone turned to stare at me—and my hand waving crazily in the air.

"Max? You changed your mind?" Coach Freeley said. "Okay, dude." He waved me toward the thick rope. "You're up first. Show 'em how it's done!"

# 6

**NICKY AND TARA GAVE** me a hard shove toward the rope. I pushed back. "I can't climb that. Are you nuts?" I cried.

Coach Freeley stared at me. "Did you just call me nuts?"

I glimpsed Traci staring at me. "Uh . . . No. I said *guts*. I'm sure I have the *guts* to climb this."

My hands were sweaty. My legs felt rubbery and weak. All eyes in the gym class were on me.

"Try not to look so frightened," Tara said.

"How can I?" I asked, a cold sweat pouring down my forehead.

"How can you *what*?" Coach Freeley asked.

"How can I make this more challenging?" I replied. "It's too easy."

"Stop talking to the rope and *climb* it," the coach said. Everyone laughed.

My hands shook as I reached up and grabbed the rope. It was thick and coarse, actually several ropes twined together. It scratched my hands as I gripped it.

"Do you have any climbing gloves?" I asked Coach Freeley.

He glared at me. "Are you going to climb it or knit a sweater with it?"

More laughter. I saw Traci shake her head.

"Stop stalling, Max. We're right here with you," Nicky said.

"Just pretend to climb," Tara said. "We'll hold on to you and carry you up to the top of the rope. No one else can see us. They'll think you're climbing."

"Make it look good," Nicky said.

I took a deep breath. The whole class was watching me. Coach Freeley had his hands on his hips and was tapping one foot impatiently.

I raised my hands. And dug my sneakers into the rope.

"Here goes," Tara said. "Hold on, Max."

They grabbed me under the arms. Then they both floated off the floor, carrying me up with them.

I scrabbled my hands over the rope, reaching one hand up over the other. And I pretended to push myself up with my feet.

Glancing down, I saw everyone staring up at me. I hoped I was making it look good. Did they believe I was really climbing?

"This is easy," I told the two ghosts.

"Easy for *you*," Tara said, groaning. "You're heavy!"

I moved higher, making climbing motions with my hands and feet. "This is awesome!" I exclaimed.

Tara groaned again, tugging me up. "You owe us big-time."

Halfway up the rope, I had a great idea.

I pulled my hands from the rope and held them straight out at my sides. "Hey, look, everyone!" I shouted at the top of my voice. *"No hands!"*

I could hear the gasps and cries of surprise down below as everyone watched me climb the rope without holding on.

"Show-off," Nicky muttered.

"I can smell that A in phys ed," I said.

"Don't worry," Tara said. "We'll find ways for you to thank us."

I grabbed the rope again and tucked my sneakers around the big knot. They floated higher and carried me to the top. I heard applause down below.

Glancing down, I saw Traci grinning up at me. Excellent! She's impressed. And I bet the no-hands thing really impressed Coach Freeley, too.

"Okay, guys," I said. "I'm ready to climb down."

I turned my head from side to side. No sign of them.

"Nicky? Tara? I'm ready for you to take me down now."

Silence.

Where were they? Was this their idea of a joke?

"Hey—not funny. Come on, guys. How do I get down?"

Below me, the gym had suddenly grown very quiet.

"Max, get your butt down here, okay?" Coach Freeley's voice broke through the silence. "Other people want a turn."

Get my butt down there? Okay. I'd love to.

But how? I didn't have a clue.

I clung to the rope. My palms began to sweat and my hands started to slip. My legs began to shake. I was losing my grip. I couldn't hold on much longer.

"Nicky? Tara? *Help!*"

# 7

**I SWALLOWED. MY THROAT** felt as dry as sawdust. I was trembling so hard, my knees were knocking together. Could everyone see that?

How could those two stupid ghosts leave me up here? I really had no idea how to get down. I knew there was no way I could slide down without ripping my whole body to pieces.

And then I realized something else—*I'm afraid of heights!*

As I gazed down, the gym started to spin. The kids, Coach Freeley, the bleachers, the gym floor—it all became a whirling blur.

Fighting off my dizziness, I raised my eyes to the ceiling. And felt my hands slip a little more. My heart pounded in my chest.

Coach Freeley is going to have to call the fire department, I thought. That's the only way I'll ever get down. But how can I hold on long enough for the firefighters to get here?

Coach Freeley turned and headed across the gym to get his clipboard. That's when I saw the ladder at the side of the gym start to move. It was a tall metal painter's ladder that had been leaning against the far wall. As I stared down, the ladder lifted itself away from the wall and appeared to move on its own—sliding toward me.

Yes—!

Kids let out startled cries as the ladder edged across the gym floor. They scrambled to get out of the way. The ladder moved past them and came to a stop at the wall beneath me.

Okay, okay, Max. This should be a piece of cake. Just hold on to the rope and lower your feet to the ladder. No prob, right?

Well, it sounded easier than it was.

I held on to the rope, lowering my hands inch by inch until my sneakers bumped the top rung of the ladder. Then slowly, slowly I lowered myself. With a final step of courage, I let go of the rope. I quickly grabbed the ladder's sides with my hands. Then I climbed down the rest of the way.

When my shoes hit the gym floor, I let out a triumphant cheer. I stopped when I realized everyone was staring hard at me.

"Max, that ladder," Traci said, pointing. "It—it walked across the gym on its own!"

Think fast, Max. Think fast.

"Of course," I said. "It's a *step*-ladder!"

Groan.

Well . . . that was the best I could do.

**34**

• • •

Up in my room that night, I waited for Nicky and Tara to appear. Why didn't they help me down the rope? I wanted to know. Why did they make me flunk the rope test?

But more important than that, I needed to tell them about Phears. I had to tell them about the Berserker Ghoul he was going to send to break me.

Break me.

I don't want to be broken, I thought, shuddering. I want my life to be normal again.

Nicky and Tara had to step up. They had to help protect me from Phears and this ghoul he was sending. After all, whose fault was it that I was in this mess?

I didn't ask to be haunted. I didn't ask for any of this. And if I was going to protect Nicky and Tara, it was only fair for them to protect me.

But where were they?

They didn't show up all night.

I tried to write in my journal. But everything I wrote about my day sounded like some kind of scary novel. No one would believe any of it. I tore out the page and promised myself I'd think of something to write tomorrow.

Finally, I tucked myself into bed, shut my eyes, and tried to forget about this awful day. But just as I started to drift off to sleep, I heard a low howl.

And then a long, shrill cry.

The cat. Again.

"Where is that cat?" I bolted up in bed.

Another low howl. Sounding so sad and lonely.

"Where are you, cat?" My muscles tensed.

Wait a minute. Maybe I'm hearing Edgar, the Swansons' black cat next door. Sometimes Edgar stands in the backyard and howls to be let inside.

I could feel my body relax. That's it, I told myself. It's just Edgar.

"*Yeeeeeeeeooooow.*"

That sad howl again. No, not Edgar. The cry was too nearby to be the Swansons' cat. "Where are you, cat? What do you want?"

Silence now.

I fell back into bed, turned onto my stomach, and pulled the blanket up to my neck. I shut my eyes and settled into the pillow.

I heard heavy footsteps. Felt a whoosh of cold air. And something leaped out of the darkness.

I tried to turn over. I tried to see what was there. But I couldn't. Something landed heavily on my back. An animal? A ghoul?

Before I could move, it grabbed my neck with two powerful claws.

# 8

"**Nooo—!**" **I LET OUT** an angry cry and tried to fight it off. Squirming and thrashing, I tugged its heavy claws off me. With a groan, I struggled onto my back.

The bedside lamp flashed on—and I gasped as I saw the creature in all its gruesome horror.

Colin. My brother, Colin.

Colin sat on top of me, fingernails still digging into my throat. Seeing my shock, he tossed back his head and laughed. His blue eyes flashed gleefully in the bright light. *"Wahoo!"* He let out a victory cry and pounded on my head for a while with both hands. He always thinks it's fun to use my head as a bongo.

"Okay. You scared me," I said. "Can I go back to sleep now?"

He grinned down at me. "Where'd you get those pajamas, Maxie?"

"What do you mean? They're my *Star Wars* pajamas. They're my favorites. I've had them forever."

"But they're torn," Colin said.

"No, they're not," I protested.

Colin grabbed my pajama shirt and ripped it down the front. "See? They're torn."

I tried to shove him off me, but he was too heavy and too strong. He works out about twenty hours a day, watching himself in a mirror the whole time. Colin loves himself, and just about everyone else does too. Because he's such a macho hunk.

Puke.

"Why'd you rip my shirt?"

"To teach you a lesson," he said.

"Excuse me? A lesson? What lesson?"

He shrugged his broad shoulders. "Beats me." He climbed off me, leaning all his weight on my ribs, and glanced around the room. "You have a cat in here, don't you, Fat Face?"

"Don't call me Fat Face. I hate that," I said.

"It's your real name. Fat Face Doyle. I saw your birth certificate."

"How funny are you, Colin? Not!"

"Where's the cat, Fat Face?"

So Colin could hear the cries too. Weird.

"I don't have a cat," I said. "What makes you think I have a cat?"

"Because I heard it meowing. It woke me up."

"Funny. I didn't hear anything," I lied.

"Maxie, if you have a cat, you're in major trouble," Colin said. "You know Mom is allergic."

38

He crossed the room to my closet and began heaving stuff out, tossing it all over the floor. "Is it in here? Where is it?"

I sat up. "Get your paws off my stuff. I told you, I don't have a cat."

What could I do? He was pulling everything out of my closet. He knows I always get into trouble with Mom and Dad when my room is a mess. I had to think of something to get him out.

"You know what I think it was?" I said. "It wasn't a cat. I think it was just my stomach growling real loud."

"Oh, really?" He backed out of the closet and turned to me. "Stomach growling? I know how to cure that, Maxie." He leaned forward, took a running start, and gave me a ferocious head-butt in the stomach.

I yelped in pain. It hurt so much, I thought his head had gone all the way *through* me!

Giggling and pumping his fists in the air, Colin ran out of the room.

A few minutes later, I started breathing again. I slid back under the covers and listened for the cat. Silence.

I knew where its cries were coming from. I think I knew all along, but I didn't want to admit it.

The cat was in the tunnel. The tunnel hidden behind a panel in my bedroom wall. Nicky and

Tara and I discovered the tunnel one night. It led to some kind of terrifying ghost world, all dark and cold and filled with lurking ghosts and spirits.

Nicky and Tara forced me to go into the tunnel to find a box of Nicky's belongings. I still have nightmares about it. I was trapped in the tunnel, trapped in the ghost world. Nicky and Tara had to pull me out, pull me back to my room.

The tunnel opening has been paneled up ever since. I never want to go back to that terrifying place again.

"Please go away," I whispered to the cat. "Please—stop crying. No one wants you here."

As I struggled to fall asleep, little did I know that I'd be pulling off that wall panel in just a few hours.

# 9

**THE NEXT MORNING, DAD** jumped up from the breakfast table as soon as I stepped into the kitchen. "Max, are you hiding a cat in your room?"

"Huh?"

That was my best reply for first thing in the morning.

I saw Colin grinning at me over his bowl of shredded wheat. Mom leaned against the kitchen counter, a mug of coffee between her hands.

"Your brother heard a cat in your room last night," Dad said.

Colin's grin grew wider. He loved getting me in trouble.

"He's a dirty liar," I said.

Mom choked on her coffee. Dad hurried over to slap her on the back. Dad is a big, beefy guy, built like a buffalo. And Mom looks sort of like a frail little bird. So when Dad slaps Mom on the back, believe me, she stops choking right away. She never wants a second helpful slap.

"Don't call your brother names," Dad said.

"Yeah. Don't call me names, you big piece of garbage," Colin chimed in.

Dad laughed at that. He thinks Colin is a riot.

"Maxie, I know you want a pet," Mom said, setting her mug on the counter. "But I'm terribly allergic to cats."

"Besides, you have Buster," Dad said.

*"Buster?"* I cried. "Buster *hates* me! He thinks I'm one of his chew toys!"

Buster is a big, furry wolfhound we got a few years ago. He stays mostly outside or in the garage. Whenever I come near him, he growls and sinks his teeth into my leg.

Dad says he's just being friendly. He says I have to get over my fear of dogs.

I'm not afraid of dogs. I'm afraid of being *eaten!*

Colin loaded his spoon with cereal and snapped it toward me. He got me right in the forehead with a big wet wad of shredded wheat.

Dad laughed. To him, everything Colin does is golden.

Mom shook her head at Colin. "Don't play with your food. And stop picking on Maxie."

"What about the cat in his room?" Colin insisted.

"Give me a break. I don't have a cat," I said through gritted teeth.

And at that moment, a loud *meeeeow* floated into the kitchen from upstairs.

Everyone froze.

And listened.

And heard another long cat cry, shrill and sad.

It's a ghost cat, I thought. It *has* to be a ghost cat. So why can everyone hear it?

This cat must *really* want to be heard!

Colin jumped up from the table. "I *told* you! Did you hear it? We *all* heard it, right?"

"Heard what?" I said. "I didn't hear anything."

But the three of them were already hurrying out of the kitchen. They went running up to my room, and I had no choice but to follow them.

What should I do? I asked myself. How can I explain this?

I decided to tell them the truth. Come clean and tell them the whole story. Then maybe they'd *finally* believe me about the ghosts in the house.

When I reached my room, Colin was tossing things out of the closet again. Dad was down on the floor, searching under the bed. Mom stood with her arms crossed, listening for the cat.

"Whoa. Stop!" I shouted. "I'll tell you the truth."

They turned to me. Mom raised her hands to her cheeks. "Oh no. Maxie, you really are hiding a cat in here?"

"It's a ghost cat," I said.

Dad and Colin groaned. "Not another crazy ghost story," Dad said. "I warned you, Max—"

"Just listen to me!" I cried. "I can prove it to you." My heart was thudding in my chest. Would I finally be able to make them believe me?

"The cat must be in the tunnel," I said.

Dad stood with his powerful arms crossed over his chest. The fire-breathing dragon tattooed on his right bicep seemed to stare at me. "What tunnel?" he asked.

"There's a tunnel in my room. It's hidden behind that wall panel." I pointed. "I just discovered it a few weeks ago. The tunnel is very long and dark. It leads to some kind of ghost world. It—"

Colin burst out laughing. "You're talking about a PlayStation game, right?"

"No, it's *true*!" I screamed.

Dad rolled his eyes. "Max, I warned you about these babyish ghost stories. . . ."

"I'll prove it!" I cried. "I'll prove it to you." I darted to the wall, wrapped my hands around the edges of the wall panel, and tugged.

Stuck.

"The tunnel is right behind this panel," I said. "You'll see."

I tugged harder.

The panel still wouldn't budge.

**44**

"You'll see," I repeated. "Then you'll be sorry you didn't believe me."

With a groan, I bent lower, tightened my hands around the edges, and yanked the panel with all my might.

"Yes!"

I pulled the panel away.

And everyone gasped.

# 10

**SOLID WALL.**

No sign of any tunnel.

I dropped the wood panel to the floor and slapped the wall with my hand. Hard plaster. I slapped at it frantically with both hands. Where was the tunnel? Where?

Mom came up from behind and put her arms around me. "Max, I'm very worried about you. Why are you making up these crazy ghost stories?"

"Because he's totally mental!" Colin exclaimed. He let out a high horse whinny. "He's gone looney tunes!"

Dad shook his head. "It isn't funny, Colin. Max needs help. I know he'll get it at the Plover School."

"Maybe you're right," Mom said. "Maybe he does need to get away from this house and go to a place with some structure."

Structure? What is *structure*?

What was she talking about? I couldn't believe it. Mom never wanted me to go away to that horrible boarding school. Why was she suddenly agreeing with Dad?

Just because the tunnel disappeared?

"You're both going to be late for school," Mom said. "We'll talk about this later. Get your backpacks and go."

I trudged across the room to get my backpack. I saw Dad staring hard at me. And the fire-breathing dragon on his arm was staring at me too.

I realized I was trembling. Now I'll never get them to believe me, I thought. I'm totally on my own—with two ghosts haunting the house. And a ghost cat. And an evil ghost who is going to bring a ghoul to break me.

Totally on my own . . .

Dear Diary,

Not much happened today.

Sorry I don't have any exciting things to write about.

I may be going to another school soon. But I don't want to write about that. Bye for now.

Max

That night, the cat appeared.

Well, it wasn't *the* cat. But it was enough of a cat to get me into major trouble.

The four of us were home having dinner. Dad brought home a bucket of chicken, and Mom microwaved some vegetables to go with it. When they weren't looking, Colin shoved a handful of string beans down the front of my shirt.

"Hey—!" I let out a shout. The string beans tickled!

That's when we heard the cat. A loud *meow* from upstairs. I glanced quickly around the table. Everyone had heard it.

I tried to make them forget about it. "I got an A on my health quiz today," I said.

But they were all listening hard. And when the cat meowed again, Dad jumped up from the table. He pointed a finger at me. "Max, I told you—no cat. No more crazy stories about a tunnel in your wall. If I find a cat up there, you're grounded for a year, maybe two."

"I don't have a cat," I protested. "Why would I hide a cat up there when I know I'm not allowed to have a cat?"

"Because you're dumb?" Colin chimed in.

"Don't call Maxie dumb," Mom said.

"He *is* dumb," Colin said. "He doesn't want to eat his string beans. So he's hiding them in his shirt."

"That's a lie!" I shouted.

But Colin jerked my shirt up out of my jeans, and the string beans tumbled out onto the floor.

"Those are *Colin's* string beans!" I cried.

Dad frowned at me. "Why did you put *Colin's* string beans down your shirt?" he asked.

Before I could answer, the cat meowed again.

And now everyone jumped up from the table and hurried to the stairs. "Hey, wait—" I called after them.

I shoved my chair back and climbed to my feet. Something crunched under my shoes. String beans. I ignored it and chased after my family.

Dad led the way up the stairs to my room. He clicked on the ceiling light, and we all jammed into the room.

"This is totally stupid," I said. "I don't know where those meows are coming from, but I don't have a cat. I swear."

"He's lying. He's definitely got a cat," Colin said, glancing around. "It has to be up here somewhere."

"I don't have a cat up here!" I cried. "I can't believe—"

Another *meow*.

We all turned toward the sound. Dad stepped up to my dresser. He pulled out the top drawer . . .

All four of us gasped as a black cat leaped out of the dresser.

# 11

**WITH A SHRILL CRY,** the cat jumped onto Dad's chest.

Startled, Dad staggered back. The cat let out a shriek and jumped to the floor. It ran through Mom's legs and darted under my bed.

Colin grinned. "Told you."

I recognized the cat instantly. It was Edgar, the Swansons' black cat from next door.

How did Edgar get in my dresser drawer? Hello. That wasn't hard to figure out.

Colin.

Had to be Big Fat Sneak Colin.

But how could I prove it?

I turned to Dad. He was steaming. Smoke didn't come out of his ears. But his face was an angry red, the color of raw hamburger. His big chest was heaving up and down like a bomb about to explode.

"Uh . . . ," I started.

Mom suddenly looked very pale. She had her hands pressed to the sides of her face. "It . . . it

50

brushed against me," she said to Dad. "Did you see? It brushed against my legs."

Then she turned to me. "Isn't that the neighbors' cat?"

"Yes," I said. "It's Edgar. I'm sure Colin—"

Mom sneezed.

Dad stormed toward me. "I don't care what its name is. Get that cat out from under your bed."

"Okay. No problem."

I dropped to my knees and pushed my head under the bed. "Edgar, it's okay. Come here," I said softly. I tried coaxing him for a while, but he didn't budge. "Edgar, *psst psst psst*. Come here, kitty. Nice kitty. You know me—right, Edgar?"

I stretched out my hands to grab him, but he was all the way back against the wall.

I heard Mom sneeze again.

And again. Loud sneezes that shook the whole bedroom.

I slid further under the bed. "Come here, Edgar. It's okay, fella. Come to Max."

I made a grab for him—and he sprang away, out into the room.

Mom let out a cry. I climbed to my feet and saw Edgar on top of my dresser. Mom opened her mouth in a violent sneeze. Her cheeks and forehead were bright red and swollen.

*"Get that cat!"* Dad screamed.

Colin moved quickly across the room. He picked up Edgar in both hands and held him against his chest. "That's a good cat," he whispered, petting Edgar's back. "What did that bad Max do to you?"

"This isn't fair!" I shouted.

Mom sneezed so hard, both of her contact lenses flew out.

Colin carried Edgar to the door. "I'll take him back where he belongs," he said. "Then I'll vacuum around here, Mom, so you'll feel better soon. I'm sure Max didn't mean to make you so sick." He disappeared down the stairs.

"But—but—but—" I sputtered.

Mom and Dad were on their hands and knees searching for Mom's contacts. "Colin is a take-charge kinda guy," Dad said to Mom.

"Colin is a take-the-cat kinda guy!" I cried. "I know you won't believe me, but he's the one who hid Edgar in my dresser drawer."

"Keeping a cat in a drawer is really cruel," Dad said. "You're grounded for life, Max. No arguments. Maybe you can go out again when you're thirty. We'll see."

I opened my mouth to protest. But I knew there was no point.

How could I ever pay Colin back for this little joke? There had to be a way.

That's what I was still thinking about late at

night when I couldn't fall asleep. How can I get my revenge? How?

And then I heard the sad *meow* of a cat. Not Edgar. The other cat, the mystery cat. A soft animal cry, so close and far away at the same time.

What else can go wrong? I asked myself.

The next morning, I found out.

# 12

**"TARA? ARE YOU HERE?"**

I blinked, trying to get used to the darkness. Where was I? How long had I been away?

"Nicky, is that you?" I heard Tara's whisper nearby.

I turned to her. Pale gray moonlight poured in from a window. Tara had a floppy hat pulled down over her hair. Her face was covered in shadow. All I could see were the long, dangling plastic earrings she always wears.

"Where are we, Nicky?"

I squinted, struggling to focus. I heard a cat meow, a soft, sad cry. "We're back in Max's room," I said. "I don't know how long we've been away."

Tara stepped into the ray of moonlight. Her expression was sad. "Think we'll ever get better at being ghosts? I hate not knowing when I'm going to appear and disappear."

The cat meowed again.

I watched Max sleeping, the blanket pulled up

over his head. He groaned in his sleep. Maybe he was having a bad dream.

Tara stepped close to me. "Something I forgot before we disappeared," she said. She slapped my arm. "Touched you last."

She scooted away. I chased after her. She tripped over Max's Darth Vader wastebasket, and it clattered to the floor. I glanced at the bed. Max didn't wake up. I tagged Tara. "Touched you last."

She slapped me back. "Touched you last."

Sometimes our "touched you last" game lasted for hours. It was a serious sport. We never wanted to be the loser. Now here we were—ghosts—and we couldn't stop playing it. Sick, huh?

Suddenly, Tara slumped down on the edge of Max's bed. She cupped her face in her hands and let out a long sigh.

"What's wrong?"

"We're nowhere, Nicky. We've been back here in our old house for weeks. And we haven't come any closer to finding Mom and Dad."

I sprawled on the floor and leaned against the bed. "That ghost named Phears is our only clue," I said. "He knows our parents. Maybe he even knows where they are. But he's too evil and too frightening. No way to talk to him."

Tara shook her head. Her earrings rattled. "We don't know how we died. And we don't know if Mom and Dad are dead or alive. We can't just sit here in our old house waiting for them to return."

"Well . . . I know," I said. "I thought your new boyfriend here was supposed to help us."

Tara bonked me on the head with her fist. "Don't call him that."

"You have a crush on Max," I said. "It's obvious."

She bonked me again, a little harder.

"Ow." Yeah, sure, I'm a ghost. But it still hurts to be bonked on the head.

Above me, Max stirred in his sleep. The cat meowed again, its voice hoarse, tired.

"Max did help a little," Tara said. "He went in the weird tunnel in the wall and brought out that box of your stuff."

"Oh, yeah. The box." I'd hidden it under the bed. I pulled it out and opened it. It had a lot of stuff I'd saved back when . . . back when I was alive.

I sifted through it. Some keys I didn't recognize . . . a Spider-Man action figure . . . a small comic book . . .

I pulled out a framed photograph of Mom and Dad and held it up to the moonlight. Tara leaned her hands on my shoulders and gazed at it with me.

"They look so young and happy," I said. Dad had an arm around Mom's shoulders. They were standing on a beach, grinning at the camera. I could see the ocean behind them. They both had wavy dark hair. Dad looked very tanned.

"I don't remember saving this photo," I said. "How did it end up in the box?"

Tara reached into the box and pulled out the red-jeweled ring. It glowed dimly, like a night-light in the dark bedroom. "The wishing ring," she murmured. "Remember? Max used it for Halloween?"

"I don't know how that ring got in the box," I said. "Did it belong to Mom and Dad? They were scientists—not magicians."

Tara slid the big ring onto her finger. The glow grew a little brighter. Under her cap, her dark eyes reflected the light. "Maybe we can make a wish, Nicky."

"Maybe," I said.

Tara raised the ring close to her face. The red glow washed over her. She stared hard at the shimmering jewel. "I wish we could find our parents." Her voice came out in a hushed whisper.

Silence now.

Tara held the ring close to her face, not taking her eyes from it. Neither one of us moved.

The light from the jewel dimmed to purple, then gray.

I realized I was still gripping the framed snapshot tightly between my hands. Suddenly, it began to vibrate.

Startled, I cried out—and dropped the photo to the carpet. I grabbed for it—and saw something flutter out of the back.

A slip of paper.

"Nicky, what is that?" Tara asked. "Did the frame break?"

I unfolded the slip of paper. "No. It's a note," I said. I held it up to the moonlight to see it better. "It's a note from Mom."

Tara dropped down beside me. "Huh? What does it say?"

# 13

**MY HANDS STARTED TO** shake. I gripped the small piece of paper tightly between them. I read the handwritten note in a trembling whisper:

"*We are very close, as close as your heart. We miss you. Find us.*"

"That's all?" Tara asked.

I turned the paper over. Nothing on the back. I turned it over again and reread the note.

"What does it mean?" Tara asked. "'As close as your heart'? Does that mean they're here in the room with us?"

I shook my head. "I don't know what it means. I guess it's some kind of clue." I picked up the photo and studied it. "'As close as your heart . . .'"

What a puzzle.

Tara grabbed the photo from me. "Maybe there are more clues inside." She started to tug off the back of the frame.

A clattering sound from downstairs made her stop. We both froze.

Max didn't seem to hear it. He was snoring lightly now, the blanket over his head.

But I heard it. Banging and scraping noises. Kitchen sounds. Someone was moving around down there.

"Lulu!" Tara cried. "Maybe Lulu is back."

She dropped the picture frame and the ring back into the box. We slid the box under Max's bed. Then we both took off, floating over the floor, flying down the stairs.

Yes, Lulu was back, standing over the stove, waving her spatula.

"Lulu! We're so happy to see you!" Tara cried. Lulu turned to hug us, and we hugged her back. Our hands went right through her.

Lulu is a ghost too. She is our old housekeeper. She is short and round, and her dark eyes glow beneath her silver-white hair, which is tied tightly on top of her head in a bun. She wore a long white apron over a loose-fitting gray blouse and a pleated skirt that hung down to the floor.

When we saw her a few weeks ago, she told us she died soon after we did, but she kept coming back to our old kitchen, waiting for us to return. We tried to ask her about Mom and Dad. But Lulu was old and weak, so she kept fading in and out.

Once again, she faded from view until only her dark eyes and the floating spatula remained. After a few seconds, we could see her again.

"Glory, glory, I've missed you," she said. "Are you getting along okay without me?"

"Not really," I said.

"Other people live in our house now," Tara told her. "A boy named Max is our friend. But the rest of his family can't see us. We can't get used to being ghosts. And we really miss Mom and Dad."

Lulu poked at invisible eggs in a frying pan on the stove. "Glory, what wonderful folks. I'd do anything for your ma and pa."

"Lulu, where are they?" I asked. "How can we find them?"

"Glory . . . glory . . ." Her voice grew faint as she faded away again.

Tara and I stood there staring at each other in the empty kitchen. Would she return?

Yes. A moment later she was back. Tara grabbed at Lulu's apron strings. "Lulu, you have to help us. Nicky, show her the note. It's from Mom. But we don't know what it means."

I held the note up close to her face. Her dark eyes slid back and forth as she read it. "Glory," she murmured. Then she flickered from view once again.

"So weak . . . Sorry, children. I'm just so weak."

"Can you help us, Lulu?" Tara begged. "Do you know what it means?"

Silence.

Then Lulu shimmered into view. "What a shock it was. What a shock when everything happened."

"But *what* happened?" I cried. "Can you tell us? What happened to us? What happened to Mom and Dad?"

"Phears," she answered in a whisper. "Your ma and pa, they captured all the ghosts. But Phears let them out. They all escaped. And then the four of you—you all disappeared."

Tara gasped. "You mean . . . You mean Phears *killed* us?"

Lulu opened her mouth to answer. But a loud cry from upstairs made her stop. The cat. We heard it again, another long, mournful howl.

Lulu gasped. Her eyes bulged wide. "I know that animal!" she exclaimed.

Tara and I stared at her. "What do you mean?"

The cat cried again.

"Yes, yes, it is." Lulu set down her spatula. She raised her eyes to the ceiling. "Phears' cat," she whispered. And then she flickered from view again.

I swallowed. My brain did a flip-flop in my head. Phears' cat was inside the house?

A few seconds later, Lulu slid back into view. "I'd recognize that cry anywhere," she said. Her eyes searched the floor. "Where is that cat? Glory, glory. Phears loved his cat more than anything.

They died together. Yes, they did. Gave up their last breaths together. Glory, I never saw a man so attached to his cat."

She picked up the spatula and stirred the invisible eggs. "Feeling weak . . . ," she whispered. "Can't stay much longer, kids. Glory, it was good to see you."

"But, Mom and Dad—" I said. "Can you help us, Lulu? Can you tell us what this note means?"

With a soft pop that sounded like a bubble bursting, she disappeared.

This time, she didn't return.

I turned sadly to my sister. "She wasn't any help," I said. "No help at all."

"Oh, yes, she was," Tara replied. "She gave me a great idea!"

# 14

**I FLEW INTO MAX'S** room inside a white moth.

I found a hole in the screen and slid right through. I'm used to slipping through small spaces. When you are an Animal Traveler, you can burrow deep or fly high. You can sail away from your enemies and come swooping back to take them by surprise.

At times, I have made myself tiny enough to ride inside a mosquito. I enjoyed the darting, shooting, jumping ride. I have soared inside broad-winged hawks. And I have crept slowly but steadily inside earthworms.

I love to move because I was kept still and in prison for so long. Captured by the Roland parents, the so-called scientists. My last ghostly breath taken from me. Held in a prison that was neither smoke nor spirit nor mirror nor air.

Phears. Phears.

My name struck terror in all who met me.

Until the Rolands took my breath and made me even *less* than a ghost.

But I escaped. My name is Phears and I had to escape. And I had to help the others float free of their prison. And now we ghosts are out. And I sail through the night inside this fluttering white insect.

Tentacles quivering. The air electric. Because I am so close . . . so close to finding the Rolands and having my revenge.

The two Roland kids—Nicky and Tara—will help me. Once I capture them, the parents will come to their rescue. And I shall have the parents, too. And then I shall destroy all four of them for-ever.

These are my thoughts as I sail through the night on this unsteady steed. And, of course, I am not alone. I have brought the jabbering Berserker Ghoul with me. What a jolly fellow he is.

He cannot sit still. He drums his hands and taps his feet and shuffles his legs up and down. A bony thing—with his shiny red top hat, red gloves, and striped jacket—rib bones poking out. What is he dressed for? Halloween? Ha, ha.

He was a normal ghoul once, rising up from his grave, staggering through the night, terrorizing people as a ghoul must do. What made him go berserk?

Was it the time I pushed away the shadows and showed him my face? He screamed for hours after that. I don't think he ever recovered.

And now he cannot keep still. He bobs his head and tugs his ears. And jabbers nonsense without stop.

Just the right fellow to teach this boy Max the difference between master and slave. Once my Berserker friend is inside Max, the boy will find himself out of control—and more terrified than any living creature before him.

I wouldn't want this drooling idiot inside *me*!

After a day or so of this ghoul's company, Max will come to me. "Please, Mr. Phears," he will whimper. "Please ask me to do *anything* for you, and I gladly will."

Ha, ha.

He's sleeping so soundly, burrowed in his bed, covers nestled over his head.

I flutter over his hair—so close I can hear his soft breaths.

Softly, softly.

Yes, go, my Berserker friend. Go do your ghoulish work. Yes, slide out of here, hopping and popping and flapping your gums. And try to stay in one place, will you?

I know you Berserkers like to hop from person to person, too jittery, too jumpy, to stay in one place. But I need you to stay inside Max. Stay long enough for Max to come begging on his knees to me. Then you may go jumping and jabbering on your way.

Do you hear me?

Can you hear me over your insane jabbering and bopping and bumping?

Go, ghoul friend. Yes, ease yourself inside his head, through the open ear canal. Yes. Yes.

Go inside and be yourself. Control the boy when he least expects it.

Go berserk.

And now, with twice as much room inside, I guide my white-winged carrier back to the window. Back out into the cool night we flutter together. Into the darkness, where I am most comfortable.

Poor Max.

What a terrifying surprise when he wakes up.

# 15

## WHERE AM I?

I woke up, blinking, shaking my head hard, trying to snap awake. My mouth felt as dry as cotton. As I lifted my head off the pillow, the room spun around me.

Whoa, Max. Get it together.

Let's start the day all over again. I shut my eyes tight, then opened them wide. Why do I feel so strange?

Oh. Of course. I wasn't in my room. I slept in Colin's room last night.

Big Jerk Colin made me trade places with him. Because Edgar, the Swansons' cat, peed in Colin's bed. So Colin took my bed, and I had to sleep in his room in the wet bed.

Actually, it wasn't bad—once I got used to the smell.

I took a very long shower, and I think I got most of the smell off my skin. Then I pulled on a pair of baggy jeans and my old Digimon T-shirt and hurried down to breakfast.

Someone had let Buster in. He growled at me from under the breakfast table. Colin was already at the table, and Mom and Dad were staring at him. "What's up?" I asked.

"There's something wrong with Colin," Mom said, biting her bottom lip.

"So what else is new?" I said. "He's a total freak."

I waited for Colin to dis me back the way he always does. But he gazed at me with a strange yellow glow in his eyes. And he said, "Jabba jabba jabba."

I laughed. "Baby talk?"

"Gubba jabba," Colin said.

"Stop doing that!" Dad screamed. "What is your problem, Colin? Why are you acting like such a jerk this morning?"

"Because he can't help it?" I said.

"Be quiet, Max. No more jokes. Your mom and I are really upset about this."

"Gubba gubba," Colin said, with that eerie yellow haze in his eyes.

"Stop it!" Dad pounded the table so hard, he knocked over all the orange juice glasses. Buster leaped out from under the table and began furiously lapping up the spilled juice.

"You're scaring us, Colin," Dad continued, glaring across the table. "It isn't funny. So stop it right now. I'm warning you."

"Jabba jabba?" Colin asked, a big dopey grin spreading across his face. And then he began honking. I mean, really. He opened his mouth wide and tossed back his head. And these unbelievable *honnnnnk*s came from deep in his throat.

"Stop it! Stop it!" Dad shouted. "Is this some kind of a game? Is it a dare? Is that what it is? Someone dared you to do this today?"

*"Honnnnnk"* was Colin's reply.

This is scary, I thought. Colin isn't playing a joke. There's something really wrong with him.

I turned and saw that Mom had tears in her eyes. She shook her head. "I don't like this, John," she said to Dad. "I don't like this one bit."

*"Heeeee-honnnnk. Heeee-honk."*

Dad turned to me. "This is the kind of stupid stunt that *you* would do. It isn't like Colin at all."

"Thanks for the compliment," I muttered. But a shiver ran down my back. I was really worried about my brother.

"Jabba gubba? Jabba jabba!"

And then we all let out cries as Colin jumped to his feet. Wailing at the top of his lungs, he began running around and around the kitchen. He swung his arms wildly and knocked over the coffeemaker. Glass shattered. A puddle of coffee spread over the floor.

Colin kept running, racing in circles, wailing

70

like an animal, flapping his arms at his sides as if he wanted to take off and fly.

"Stop him! Stop him!" Mom screamed. She grabbed Dad by the waist and held on to him. "Can't you do something?"

"Not with you holding on to me, Harriet."

Buster barked his head off. Even he knew something was wrong.

I stared in shock. I couldn't move. Why was Colin doing this? Why was he going totally berserk?

As we stared in horror, Colin ran headfirst into the refrigerator. He bounced off, tumbled to the floor, and did some weird spinning moves on the floor like really bad break dancing.

"Jabba gubba jabba gubba!"

He picked himself up, slammed himself into the front of the oven, bounced off, and then ran around the kitchen counter, flapping his arms like a bird.

"Do something!" Mom screamed. "He's gone crazy! *Do* something!"

# 16

**FINALLY, DAD GRABBED COLIN** around the chest and forced him to stop. Dad is built like a truck. He has big, powerful arms, and he held on to Colin, held him in place and wouldn't let him take another step.

"Jabba," Colin said. But it came out in a weak whisper. "Jabba."

And then my brother seemed to collapse. He just folded up with Dad holding him. And I thought I saw the yellow glow fade from Colin's eyes. A sound floated from his throat like air escaping a balloon.

I felt a whoosh of air over me. It fluttered my hair. And I felt a breeze pushing lightly against the side of my face, like someone blowing into my ear.

Weird.

"Colin?" Dad asked breathlessly. His face was bright red. His muscles bulged as he held on to my brother. "Colin? Are you finished?"

Mom stood next to me, trembling. Tears rolled down her cheeks. "Colin? Are you okay?"

"Yeah. Fine," he said in his normal voice. "What's up?"

Dad slowly let go of him. "At least he's speaking again," he said to Mom.

"Speaking? Why wouldn't I speak?" Colin asked, confused. He raised his eyes to me. "What's up with this, Maxie? What did you do to me?"

"Hey—no way," I said. "No way you're blaming me."

"Blaming you for what?" Colin asked, scratching his head. I don't think he remembered anything.

"You just went totally berserk," I told him. "Look at this kitchen. You did all that."

Blinking as if he was just waking up, Colin gazed around the room. "Wow. What a mess."

"You were running around the room, acting totally wacko," I said.

Colin squinted at me. "Yes. I kinda remember now. I wasn't in control. I couldn't stop myself. Did you hypnotize me? Is that what made me do it? You and your crazy magic tricks. Did you hypnotize me?"

Mom and Dad turned their eyes on me.

"Hel-lo. Did I go near you this morning?" I said. "I don't think so." They were always ready to blame me. "I just do simple tricks," I said. "I don't know how to hypnotize anyone."

"I think we need to get Colin to Dr. Welles'

office," Mom said. She felt his forehead. "Do you have a fever?"

"No, Mom." Colin pulled away. "I feel fine now. I don't need a doctor."

"But how do you explain your behavior?" Dad asked, scratching his bald head.

Colin shrugged. "I just felt strange. Like I was sleepwalking or something."

That answer seemed okay to Mom and Dad. Mom bent down and started to pick up the broken glass from the coffeemaker. "Better hurry to school, boys. It's very late."

I picked up my backpack and ran to the front closet to get my jacket. As I slid into the jacket, I glimpsed myself in the mirror on the closet door.

That wasn't a yellow glow in my eyes—*was* it?

No. It must have been sunlight reflecting from the living room window.

# 17

I MET AARON IN the hall at school. Aaron has long curly red hair and freckles. Teachers always tell him he looks like Huck Finn. But we don't know if that's good or bad.

Aaron wears baggy brown cargo shorts to school every day. He even wears shorts on the coldest, snowiest days of the winter.

Why?

He says, "No reason."

But I know the reason—it's because he thinks he has great-looking legs.

One of the other weird things about Aaron is that he never does his schoolwork. He says he comes to school to learn things, not to do a lot of work.

Mom and Dad don't want me to hang around with Aaron. They say he's a bad influence. But I don't think he's an influence at all. I think he's just a good friend.

"What are you doing for after-school?" Aaron asked.

After-school? I totally forgot. We have a new program at Jefferson Elementary. Twice a week we have to stay after school and do some activity.

I sighed. "I got signed up for soccer."

Aaron shook his head. "You'll get creamed."

"I know," I said. "Colin makes me practice soccer with him in the backyard. Mainly, he uses me for target practice. He just keeps kicking the ball at me until I'm a five-foot-four bruise."

Aaron patted me on the shoulder. "Dude. This afternoon. Bring a lot of Band-Aids."

We started toward Ms. McDonald's class. "What are you doing for after-school?" I asked.

"Internet chess."

"Excuse me?" I stopped him. "You don't play chess, remember?"

"I know. But I can just pretend I'm planning my next move and stare at the screen till it's time to go home."

See? Aaron's got it all worked out.

We stepped into the classroom. Traci Wayne looked up when I walked in. She quickly lowered her eyes to the book she was reading.

I glanced toward the front. Ms. McDonald wasn't there. Kids were perched on the windowsills, laughing and talking. A couple of guys were heaving a lunch box back and forth across the room, playing keep-away from another boy. Robby Marx was showing off some new kind of dance move, making hip-hop beats with his mouth.

Giggling, two girls chased a boy, pinned him to the chalkboard, and grabbed a notebook from his hand. "Give it back!" he screamed, and chased them to the back of the room.

Justin Freed, the kid who sits next to me in the back row, slapped me a hard high five. "What's up, Max?"

Before I could answer, Ms. McDonald stepped into the room. She is my favorite teacher of all time. She is very young and very cool-looking. She always wears sweaters and faded jeans to school. She has bright blue eyes, long, curly black hair, and an awesome smile.

But she wasn't smiling this morning. She was holding her head with both hands. "Quiet, please!" she shouted. "Quiet! I mean it. Quiet!"

The two boys gave the lunch box one last toss. The kids on the windowsills jumped off and slid into their seats. The girls gave the boy his notebook back and hurried to sit down.

"I have a splitting headache this morning," Ms. McDonald said, groaning. Still holding her head, she dropped into her desk chair. "I don't want to hear a cough or a whisper or a pin drop. I need total silence."

Traci raised her hand. "Aren't we going to read our book reports?"

Ms. McDonald shook her head. "We're not going to do anything out loud. We're going to have quiet reading—*very* quiet reading until my headache goes away. Everyone understand? Don't say yes. Just nod."

We all nodded. Then there was a lot of soft chair scraping and backpack rustling as we all pulled out books for quiet reading.

Holding her head, Ms. McDonald stared down at her desk. Everyone started to read. The room grew silent, so silent I could hear birds chirping outside.

"Very good, class," Ms. McDonald said. "Thank you for your cooperation."

And that's when I suddenly went berserk.

# 18

**BEFORE I EVEN REALIZED** it, I jumped from my seat. I pumped my fists in the air and let out a deafening cry.

Ms. McDonald gasped and squinted across the room at me. "Max? What are you doing?"

I let out another high scream.

I couldn't answer her question. I didn't know *what* I was doing.

I only knew I wasn't in control.

"Sit down, Max. That's not funny," the teacher groaned, holding her head.

"Gubba hubbba?" I said. "Gubbba gubbba hubbba!"

Why was I jabbering like that?

I wanted to sit down. But I couldn't. I took off, running around the room, flapping my arms like a bird.

"*Whooooooeeeee!*" I opened my mouth in an endless scream.

When I reached the front of the room, I did a high cartwheel. (I'd never done a cartwheel in my life!) As I came down, I kicked over the trash can with both feet. It banged noisily against the wall and rolled into Ms. McDonald's desk.

"Max—control yourself!" she screamed.

But I couldn't. I turned another cartwheel. Then I cut the air with a few karate kicks. I circled the room twice, running wildly. As I ran, I grabbed the paintings and posters off the walls and tossed them behind me on the floor.

Kids were gasping and screaming. I saw Traci gaping at me in horror, her mouth dropped open to her knees! Aaron looked a bit confused too.

"Ohhh, my headache . . . ," Ms. McDonald groaned. "Somebody—stop him!"

I banged my head on the chalkboard. I spun away, up to Ms. McDonald's desk.

I can't stop! Help me! I can't stop!

That's what I *wanted* to scream. But instead, it came out, "Jabba jabbba gummma!"

And then, to my horror, I turned my back to Ms. McDonald. I stuck out my butt and started to shimmy and shake it like a dancer in an MTV hip-hop video.

That got everyone laughing and screaming.

Ms. McDonald shot around her desk and grabbed me by the arms. "Stop it, Max. Stop it!"

But I was still shimmying and shaking my butt when Mrs. Wright, the principal, stepped into the room.

Her mouth dropped open, and a loud gurgling noise came from her throat. Her face turned purple with anger. "Are we having dancing lessons?" she finally choked out. "What is all the uproar in this room?"

"I . . . uh . . . I'm just practicing for the homecoming dance," I said.

*Hey!* I could talk again!

And I had stopped shimmying. My heart pounded like a drum in my chest. Sweat poured down my face. I felt dizzy. But at least I had stopped going crazy.

"Max is having a problem this morning," Ms. McDonald explained. She turned to me. "Max, what on earth—?"

"I . . . I can explain," I stammered.

Everyone in the room stared at me. I wiped sweat off my forehead with my T-shirt sleeve.

"You'd better have a good explanation for going wild like that," Mrs. Wright said.

"Yes. I have a very good explanation," I said, still catching my breath.

And I did. I knew exactly what my problem was. I was possessed.

I didn't forget the threat that Phears had made. He promised to bring a Berserker Ghoul to ruin my life. He said the ghoul would drive me crazy. Phears said I would beg him to get rid of it, even if it meant becoming Phears' slave.

Well, Phears had kept his promise.

Now I also knew what was wrong with Colin this morning. The ghoul possessed Colin first because he was sleeping in my bed. Then it probably realized its mistake.

But it was inside me now. I could feel it in there, making my arms and legs heavy. Making my muscles twitch. Putting a yellow tint on everything I saw.

What should I do?

I decided to tell the truth.

"Mrs. Wright, please let me explain," I said in a shaky voice. "I'm really sorry I freaked out. But I can't help it. I'm possessed by some kind of ghoul. It's called a Berserker Ghoul, and it took over my body and made me go berserk. I had no control at all."

Breathing hard, I stared at her. "Do you believe me? Please say you believe me."

Mrs. Wright stared back at me. Holding her head, Ms. McDonald stared at her. The kids were all staring at me too. Except for Aaron, who stared out the window.

"Do you believe me? *Do* you?"

"Of course I believe you," Mrs. Wright said. "It makes perfect sense to me."

# 19

"**I ALSO BELIEVE THAT** SpongeBob can really talk underwater," Mrs. Wright said. "And of course I believe that Superman can fly in real life."

I swallowed. "Oh. I get it."

"Yes, you *are* going to get it," Mrs. Wright said, taking me by the arm. "Unless you have a better explanation."

"Uh . . . would you believe too many Cocoa Puffs for breakfast? You know. All that sugar."

"Sorry. Come with me."

She half pulled, half dragged me to her office. "Max, are you back again?" Ms. Harold, the assistant principal, asked.

"It's all a big mistake," I said.

Mrs. Wright led me into her office and pointed to the couch at the far wall. "Have a seat, Max. In a moment, you and I will have a nice long chat."

I dropped down onto the couch. Mrs. Wright stood at her desk, sifting through a stack of pink phone messages.

My mind raced. What could I tell her?

I needed a better explanation. Something better than the truth. Of course she didn't believe I was possessed by a ghoul. Who would believe *that*? I needed something simpler.

And at that instant, Nicky and Tara appeared. "Hi, Max." They both waved and sat down on the edges of Mrs. Wright's desk.

"What are *you* doing here?" I asked.

"It's my office," Mrs. Wright said. "Why wouldn't I be here?"

"Sorry we haven't been around," Nicky said. "We've been out searching for clues about Mom and Dad."

"We need your help, Max," Tara said.

"I can't help you now," I said.

"I don't need help," Mrs. Wright said. "I'm just looking through all these phone messages."

Tara slid off the desk and tugged my hand. "Come on, Max. Nicky and I want to show you something."

"Let go of me!" I said.

Mrs. Wright looked up from her messages. "Excuse me?"

"Uh . . . a very big mosquito," I said. "It wouldn't let go of my hand." I gave my hand a hard slap. "There. Got it."

"We found a note from our mother," Nicky said. "You've got to help us figure out what it means."

"Can't you see I'm a little busy?" I said.

Mrs. Wright slammed the messages onto her desktop and glared at me. "Max, I'm being very patient with you, but—"

"Come on. Come on." Tara tugged me again. "We need you more than she does."

"Come with us, Max. Hurry." Nicky pulled me by my other hand.

"Please—just shut up!" I cried.

"Okay, that does it," Mrs. Wright said through gritted teeth. "I'm calling your parents."

Mrs. Wright and I then had a very long chat. She did most of the talking. She wanted to know why I went berserk in class, and I couldn't think of anything to tell her.

"Maybe you are sick," she said at one point. "Your eyes look a little yellow."

Those aren't my eyes. Those are the ghoul's eyes.

That's what I wanted to say. But I just nodded and kept my mouth shut. I begged her not to call my parents.

"Since you don't have an explanation, I need to talk to them," she replied. "I just want to help you, Max."

Yeah. You're helping me right into the Plover School.

The rest of my day was pretty tense. My

stomach gurgled and growled. I felt kind of shivery, kind of tingly.

I knew the reason—I was possessed. I kept waiting for the ghoul inside me to start his act again. All afternoon, I gripped the top of my desk and prayed I didn't leap up and go crazy.

But the ghoul must have been sleeping or something.

After school, I wanted to hurry home and talk to Nicky and Tara. Maybe somehow they could help me get this ghoul out.

But I had after-school soccer, and I didn't want to get into more trouble by cutting it.

I stepped out of the school building into a blustery, gray day with dark clouds low overhead. I zipped my jacket and leaned into the wind.

I could see some kids already kicking a ball around on the soccer field. I hate soccer. I always trip over the ball. Or else I get bonked in the head.

I sighed. Oh, well. Go do it, Max.

But then, as I crossed the playground, a huge hand poked up from under the ground and grabbed me by the ankle.

# 20

**THE HAND TRIED TO** grip my leg.

I let out a scream.

Several kids looked up from the soccer field to see what the problem was.

I glanced down. A glove. *Not* a hand from under the grass. A brown leather glove.

Ha, ha. The joke's on me, huh? Someone dropped it on the playground. And the wind blew it against my leg.

Max, get it together, dude. You've got *enough* problems without imagining more!

I took a moment to catch my breath. Then I tossed the glove aside and continued jogging to the soccer field.

I saw four or five guys from the Jefferson team kicking a ball back and forth, warming up. Several other kids were there, doing stretching exercises, jogging in place, shoving each other, goofing around.

Coach Freeley stood at the sidelines in a T-shirt and track shorts, ignoring the cold weather like the macho guy he is. I saw Traci Wayne and two of her friends sitting in the bleachers watching the guys practice.

I waved to Traci, but she didn't wave back.

"Hey, here comes Brainimon!" someone shouted.

"Brainimon! Brainimon! Brainimon!" a few kids started to chant.

"Okay, who wants Max on their team?" Coach Freeley called out. He blew his whistle to stop the Brainimon chant. "Who wants Max?"

No hands went up.

"Come on," Coach Freeley shouted. "Someone has to take him."

No hands.

Coach shook his head. "Okay. I'm going to assign him to Jared's team."

Jared and everyone on his team groaned. That didn't bother me. I'm used to it. I trotted over to Jared. "Where do you want me to play?"

"How about in Canada?"

Jared's a very funny guy.

"Just try to stay out of the way," he said.

I nodded. "No problem."

The game started, and I stayed as far away from the ball as possible. As I ran back and forth, trying to look as if I was really into it, I kept glancing at Traci on the bleachers.

If only I could make one awesome play that would really impress her.

Near the end of the match, I got my wish.

The score was tied, 1 to 1. So far, I'd managed to play the whole match without touching the ball once.

With only a minute to go, I felt something move inside me. My stomach tightened. I thought I just had to burp. But a loud scream shot out of my throat.

I had been running a few yards behind Jared. As I let out my roar, I lowered my shoulder and bumped him hard from behind. Jared stumbled and fell to the ground.

Out of control. I was out of control again.

Helpless. Nothing I could do. No way to stop myself.

I kicked the ball away from Jared. Lowered my head and gut-butted a kid trying to block me. He howled and grabbed his stomach. I moved the ball past him. Kicked it through the legs of another guy. Sent him sprawling with a fist in the chest.

Other players watched in horror. A girl tried to block my path and I ran right over her. She landed hard on her backside and bounced twice. And I moved in toward the goal.

Luke West was goalie for the other team. Luke is big and mean. He's one of the stars of the real

Jefferson soccer team. He spread out his arms and tensed his back, ready for my kick.

No way could he be ready.

I opened my mouth in a deafening roar. And kicked the ball so hard, it *exploded*. The shredded soccer ball sailed over Luke's head, into the net.

*Gooooooaaaaaaaal!*

Game over. Kids on my team began to cheer. Someone slapped me on the back. The chant began again: "Brainimon! Brainimon! Brainimon!"

Did I feel happy?

No way. I just wanted help. *I wasn't in control of my own body!*

"Brainimon, how did you do that?" Jared asked, trotting up beside me.

"Jabba jabbba gummma," I said.

He laughed. "You were great, dude!"

"Gummma jabba!"

I felt an arm on my shoulder. I turned to see Coach Freeley grinning at me. "Way to show some fighting spirit, Max. Good aggressive play. I liked your enthusiasm."

"Jabba?"

"I need you on the team," Coach Freeley said, his arm around my shoulder. "Come to practice tomorrow, okay? You'll start in our game on Saturday. You'll be our secret weapon."

"Huh? Wabbba?"

He held up the torn soccer ball and shook his

head. "Good work, Max. You're going to be a star!"

*But it isn't me!* I wanted to shout. I can't play soccer. I can't be the star of the team!

I need *help*!

I turned and started to jog off the field. My eyeballs burned. I knew my eyes were glowing bright yellow. The ghoul felt heavy inside me. As I trotted away, my legs suddenly felt as if they weighed a thousand pounds.

"Hubbba hubbba hubba," I muttered in a deep voice—*not my voice!*

Please go away! I thought. Please leave me alone.

How could I get rid of this ghoul? I knew there was only one way to remove it. Help Phears. Bring Nicky and Tara to Phears. Then Phears would send his ghoul friend away.

Could I do it? No way.

Nicky and Tara are my friends. I couldn't turn traitor and hand them over to that evil ghost.

Did that mean I was stuck with the Berserker for the rest of my life? If I didn't cooperate, would Phears send something *worse*?

That idea made me shudder.

I turned and saw Traci Wayne running after me, her blond hair flying in the wind. She came bursting up and slapped me a high five. "You were *awesome*, Max!" she said.

Whoa. Traci Wayne actually *touched* me?

Maybe life wasn't so bad after all.

Traci grinned at me. "I didn't know you were so strong. Have you been secretly practicing or something?"

Please, ghoul—let me speak. Please don't mess this up for me!

"Jabbba hubbba hubbba."

Traci narrowed her eyes at me. "Excuse me?"

"Jabbba gummma."

"Your brother plays soccer, right?" Traci asked. "Colin is like the big star for the middle school, right?"

"Hubbbba gubbbba."

I wanted to be cool. I really did. This was my big moment. My one big chance to impress Traci.

But I couldn't help myself. I started bending my knees, bouncing up and down really fast like a monkey. And then I twirled around in a circle—*and I licked her face!*

Oh no. Oh noooooooo. Oh no. Oh no.

I licked Traci Wayne's face.

"Eeuuuuw." She pulled back in horror. "Max, you're so gross. You're a total freak!" She spun away and went running back to her friends.

Was she going to tell them what I did?

My life was over. I knew Traci would never speak to me again. And once word got around school that I licked her face, kids would be laughing at me for the rest of the year. Maybe the rest of my life.

I couldn't help it. I was possessed by a ghoul. What could I do?

# 21

I CALLED AARON AS soon as I got home. "I have to talk to you," I said breathlessly. "Listen to me, please. Before I go berserk again."

"Yeah. You were weird in class this morning," Aaron said. "What was up with all that running around the room?"

"That's what I'm trying to explain," I said. "I think you're the only one who will believe me."

"How was your after-school thing?" Aaron asked. I could hear him crunching on something. He likes to eat an entire bag of pistachios before dinner. He says it helps his appetite.

I know he's weird, but he's all I've got.

"I knocked everyone down and kicked the winning goal," I said.

He laughed. "In your dreams, dude."

"No. Really—" I protested.

"Internet chess is way cool," Aaron interrupted. "I could really get into it."

"Did you win?" I asked.

"I didn't move," Aaron replied. "I sat there the

whole hour planning my first move. Then I went home."

"Cool." I could hear Colin clomping up the stairs. I quickly closed my bedroom door. I sat down on the edge of my bed. "Aaron, you've got to listen to me. I'm not making this up. I've been possessed by a thing called a Berserker Ghoul."

Silence at the other end. Then he finally said, "Really?"

"Yeah. Really. That's why I went nuts this morning. It wasn't me. It was the ghoul."

Silence again. I knew Aaron was thinking hard about this. "Which movie is this? I forget," he said.

"I'm not describing a movie, Aaron. It's my life. An evil ghost sent this ghoul to destroy me so that I'll beg the ghost to let me help him."

Would Aaron believe me? He was my best friend. He *had* to believe me, right?

Aaron burst out laughing. "Awesome," he said. "Are you writing this stuff in your journal? Ms. McDonald will totally spaz out. Hey, maybe I'll write that ghoul idea too. Oh, wow. Wouldn't that be ultracool if you and I handed in our journals and they were both exactly the same?"

He cackled at that idea for nearly five minutes.

"Uh . . . Aaron?" I had the feeling that maybe I wasn't getting through to him.

"Mom's calling me," Aaron said. "Dinnertime. We're having SpaghettiOs. You know. All those little Os. I try to spell words with them. Later, dude. Let's work on our journals tonight." He hung up.

I stared at the phone, shaking my head. Then I angrily heaved it at the wall. It bounced hard and landed on my pillow.

"Take it easy," Nicky said. He and Tara appeared suddenly on either side of me. "You're totally stressed."

"Of *course* I'm totally stressed," I snapped. "This ghoul is going to ruin my life. And even my best friend won't believe me."

"We believe you, Maxie," Tara said. She wrapped her hand around the bullet-shaped silver pendant I wear around my neck. She tucked the pendant into my T-shirt. "You're all sweaty. You've really got to relax."

"How can I relax?" I screamed. "Any moment, I might go berserk again. I never know when this thing is going to wake up. I'm not in control of my own body. Do you know what that feels like?"

Nicky lowered his eyes. "Tara and I don't *have* bodies," he said softly.

"We're not talking about you," I said. "We're talking about me. You got me into this mess. What am I going to do about this ghoul? I know Phears

96

is going to leave him inside me until I turn you two in."

Tara shrugged. "No problem."

I stared at her. "Huh? No problem?"

"I have a plan," Tara said, her dark eyes flashing. "A perfect plan. We can get Phears to take that ghoul away. Easy."

I jumped to my feet. "Well? Maybe you'd like to share it with me?"

Before she could answer, my bedroom door swung open and Colin strode in. The ghosts vanished. Colin glanced around. "Hey, Fat Face, who were you talking to?"

"Uh . . . well . . ."

"I heard you talking to someone," Colin said. "Who was it?"

"I was . . . uh . . . talking on the phone," I said.

He squinted at me. "The phone? But . . . the phone is way over there on your bed."

"Yeah, I know," I said. "I was talking *long distance*."

He squinted harder at me. "Mom says to come downstairs for dinner," he said.

I followed him into the kitchen. Dad was already at the table, tossing the salad. Mom turned from the oven when I came in. "Max, I got a call from Mrs. Wright at school this afternoon."

"It's all a big misunderstanding," I said.

"Ooh, big word for such a little man," Colin said. He rolled up his dinner napkin and snapped it at me, hitting me in the forehead.

"She wants to see your dad and me at school," Mom continued.

"I didn't do it. Really," I lied.

Dad growled at me. "I warned you, Max . . ."

"Hey, I've got some *good* news," I said. "Guess what, Dad? Coach Freeley asked me to be on the soccer team. I'm going to start the game on Saturday."

A smile crossed Dad's face. "Hey, another soccer star in the family!" He reached across the table to slap me a high five. "I'm gonna have *two* all-stars in the family!"

"You're lying, right?" Colin asked, grinning at me. "You just wanted to change the subject?"

"Coach *begged* me to join the team," I told Dad. "I'm starting practice tomorrow afternoon."

Dad grinned at me. "I *knew* you weren't a helpless, pathetic wimp!"

I grinned back at Dad. "Thanks for the compliment."

Colin grinned at me. "I know you're lying."

We all grinned at each other.

"Pass the salad," Mom said, joining us at the table. "I don't know why everyone is grinning. Max is in big trouble in school again, and I just don't know what to do."

"Give the kid a break," Dad said, heaping meat loaf on his plate. "He has to concentrate on soccer now."

Wow. Can you believe it? Dad actually taking my side?

Things were definitely looking up. I spooned potatoes onto my plate, then took the meat loaf platter from Dad. I was feeling pretty happy.

But then I felt something stir inside me.

Something shifted in my brain. And I suddenly knew what I was going to do. I was going to heave the meat loaf platter against the wall. Then I was going to pick up everyone's dinner plate and toss them, too.

Oh, wow. I can't stop myself. I feel myself slipping out of control.

Here goes . . .

"Jabba jabba gumma!"

# 22

**THE NEXT MORNING, MOM** called the school and said I'd be late. Then she took me to see Dr. Welles.

Dr. Welles has an office with two other doctors in a bright new building a few blocks from the mall. He is a nice young doctor with long blond hair that always falls in front of his eyes when he examines you. He seems like a really cool guy, and I'm sure he's a good doctor. I mean, he's got a lot of certificates on his wall.

But what can a doctor do about a Berserker Ghoul?

"Maybe you need vitamins or something," Mom said as she pulled our car into the parking lot. "Maybe your system is missing something." She kept chewing her bottom lip and looking really worried. "Maybe you do need to change schools and get away for a while."

Oh, wow.

Last night, it took nearly an hour to clean up the mess I made throwing all the food against the kitchen wall. Mom and Dad both grabbed me and hugged me till I calmed down. Even Colin looked worried.

I felt so bad. Once I could talk again, I apologized over and over. Mom was sure Dr. Welles would find out what was wrong with me.

And now here I was wearing one of those crinkly blue paper robes. Sitting on his examining table while he poked his cold stethoscope against my chest and made me take deep breaths.

His hair fell over his eyes as he leaned down to study my face. "Your eyeballs look a little yellow," he said softly.

That's because there's a ghoul looking out my eyes, Doc.

I didn't say it. I wanted to say it. But what would be the point?

"We'll do a blood test. Check for hepatitis," he said. He smiled at me. "Hey, Max, did you hear about the really dumb guy who stayed up all night studying for his blood test?"

"Ha, ha." I tried to laugh. But every time I remembered last night . . . every time I thought about the ghoul inside me . . . I didn't want to laugh. I wanted to scream. Or cry.

After I got dressed, Mom met me in Dr. Welles' office. She sat down across from his desk and clasped her hands tightly in her lap. "Well? What do you think, Doctor?"

"Everything checks out okay," Dr. Welles told her, brushing back his hair. "Maybe Max should get more exercise."

Exercise?

I have a gross jabbering ghoul inside my body—and he wants me to get more exercise?

A few minutes later, Mom and I were driving home. Mom patted my head. "Do you feel any better, Maxie?"

"Oh, yes," I lied. "I feel a lot better, Mom."

I'll feel better—until the ghoul wakes up and makes me go berserk again. I suddenly felt really sorry for myself. The ghoul had jumped from Colin to me. Now wasn't it someone else's turn? Why didn't it jump to someone else?

*Because Phears wants it inside* you.

I answered the question myself.

*Because Phears wants to* break *you.*

Well, I felt pretty much broken. Where was Phears, anyway? We drove past two fat brown rabbits on a front lawn, and I shuddered. Phears could be inside one of those rabbits.

Phears could be coming back for me at any time. . . .

Mom pulled the car up the driveway. "I'll wait in the car," she said. "Run upstairs and get your backpack. Then I'll drive you to school."

I ran up to my room and found my backpack at the side of my bed. The cat in the wall was crying again. I banged my fist on the wall. "Go away! Go away!"

"Don't scare it away, Max!" a voice cried. I turned to see Nicky and Tara on the edge of my bed.

"The cat is driving me crazy," I said.

"But we need it," Tara said. She pulled me over to my desk chair. "Sit down. I want to tell you my plan."

"I can't," I told her. "Mom is waiting for me in the car."

"But my plan is so simple," Tara said. "It won't take long to explain."

"We need that cat," Nicky said, pointing to the wall. "It's Phears' cat."

I swallowed. "You're kidding me, right? Why do we need Phears' cat?"

"Because we can make a deal with him," Tara said.

"Make a deal with that evil ghost?"

Nicky and Tara both nodded. "Lulu told us Phears loves his cat more than anything. So we make a deal. We'll give Phears his cat—*if* he'll send the Berserker Ghoul away. *And* if he'll tell us what he knows about our mom and dad."

I stared at them, thinking hard. Make a deal with Phears? "Well . . . it might work," I said.

The cat meowed again, a mournful sound.

"There's only one problem," I continued. "How do we get the cat?"

"That's no problem," Nicky said.

"Yeah. No problem," Tara agreed. "It will be easy. You go in the tunnel and bring it out."

# 23

SATURDAY TURNED OUT TO be a chilly, gray November afternoon. I could see my breath steam up in front of me as I trotted across the grass to the soccer field behind school.

Some of the guys on our team were already warming up, doing stretching exercises, kicking soccer balls back and forth. I saw the visiting team's school bus pull up to the teachers' parking lot. The Terrible Tiger Cubs were here to play. Everyone said they were the best elementary school team in town.

A small crowd had gathered at the bleachers to watch the game. Traci Wayne sat at the top with some of her cool friends. She waved to me, and I waved back and shouted hi. Then I realized she was waving to Robby Marx, who was coming up behind me.

I tossed my jacket onto the pile of jackets on the bench and picked up a yellow and white Battling Bulldogs team jersey. When I looked up, I saw my dad at the sidelines, waving for my attention. "Kill 'em, Max!" he shouted. "Kill 'em! Break 'em apart! *Kill* 'em, boy!"

Dad isn't exactly what you'd call a good sport.

Colin stood beside Dad, hands stuffed in his jacket, a big grin on his face. He expected me to totally mess up, and I knew he was probably right.

The sky grew darker. Black clouds rolled overhead. I shut my eyes and prayed the game would be rained out.

When I opened them, Coach Freeley was standing in front of me, a big grin on his face. "You're our secret weapon, Max," he said, slapping me on the back. "No one expects you to be the *monster* you are!"

"Uh . . . thanks, Coach."

"Get out there, Max. Be aggressive. Be a *monster*!" He slapped me on the back again, then turned and trotted off to greet the visiting team.

Be a monster.

Great advice.

My whole body shuddered. What if I got out on the field and the Berserker Ghoul didn't take over like the other day? The ghoul had been sleeping for days. What if it decided to keep on sleeping and left me stranded out there on my own?

I can't play soccer. I'll get *creamed*!

Feeling panic sweep over my body, I glanced around. "Nicky? Tara? Are you here?"

Where were they? They promised to be here. They promised to help me during the game.

"Nicky? Tara?"

I couldn't believe they weren't here. How could they do this to me?

We'd made a deal. They help me look like a good soccer player on the field. And I risk my life and go back into that terrifying tunnel and carry out Phears' cat.

The whistle blew for us to line up. The match was about to begin.

I turned and saw Dad shaking his fists in the air. "*Kill* 'em, Max! *Break* 'em! *Kill! Kill!*"

# 24

**THE MATCH STARTED. I** tried to stay away from the ball. But my teammates kept passing it to me. They expected me to go berserk, knock players onto their butts, charge the net, and score—the way I did in that crazy practice.

But the Berserker Ghoul was still asleep.

It was just me—me all by myself out there—and I totally sucked. A couple of times, I tripped over the ball and went sailing onto my stomach on the hard ground. Once, the ball bounced right through my legs. Three times, I tried to take a shot—and kicked the ball *behind* me instead of in front of me!

Yikes.

After a few more stumbles and missed kicks, Coach Freeley took me out of the game and sent in Robby Marx. "What's wrong, Max?" Coach asked, leading me to the bench. He slapped a water bottle into my hand. "You saving it for the end again? That's okay. Take a breather. Don't forget. You're my secret weapon."

Yeah. I'm the secret weapon. And so far, I was keeping it *really secret*!

I glanced up to the top of the bleachers. Traci Wayne was cheering for the team. I sure hadn't given her anything to cheer about. She'll never talk to me now, I thought. None of the cool kids will ever talk to me.

My dad was still standing on the sidelines, silent now, hands balled into fists at his sides. Colin had that obnoxious grin on his face. Suddenly, he turned to me and mouthed the word *loser*.

Despite the cold weather, sweat poured down my forehead. "Nicky? Tara? Are you here?" I called.

Where *were* they? They promised!

Three minutes left to play. The Battling Bulldogs were losing 2 to 1. Cold raindrops started to drip down from the black sky.

I sat shivering on the bench. A hand squeezed my shoulder. I looked up to see Coach Freeley, clipboard in one hand. "Get in there, Max," he growled. "Go crazy."

"Jabbba gummma gumma," I said.

Yes!

I felt the ghoul shift inside me. The field took on a yellow glow, bright as sunshine. My feet pounded the ground, but I felt as if I was floating.

"Jabbbba hubbbba!" A battle cry roared out of my open mouth.

I head-butted one player and sent him tumbling to the wet ground. Oh, wow. One of *our* players!

I bumped a Tiger Cub out of the way. Kicked him hard in the leg. Stole the ball from him and moved it toward the goal.

Another roar escaped my throat. I could see the startled faces of my teammates. And I could hear my dad over the shouts of the crowd: "Kill! Kill! *Kill!*"

I faded away into a yellow cloud as the Berserker Ghoul totally took over my brain and my body. I felt so helpless . . . so *alone* inside my own body!

I felt jolt after jolt as the ghoul banged into the other players, bumped them hard and sent them sprawling onto the grass. I heard cries all around me and felt another hard bump as my shoe sent the ball flying—*into the net!*

And then I went crashing through the net. I stood roaring, ripping the net to pieces.

The shouts of the crowd broke through the yellow haze. And I was back. Yes. It was me again. My teammates were crowding around me, slapping me high fives, pounding my back.

I had tied up the game with less than five seconds to go. The Terrible Tiger Cubs were going home without a victory. And once again, Max the Monster had triumphed.

Traci Wayne ran up and slapped me on the shoulder. "Max, you're the *man*!"

Did she really say that? Or was my imagination running away from me? Traci Wayne wouldn't say that to *me*—would she?

Dad wrapped me in a bear hug, so tight my tongue popped out of my mouth. I expected him to say something about how proud he was or how surprised. But instead, his words filled me with dread:

"They need you at the Plover School, Max. You'll be a superstar at that school!"

No. Oh no.

All my fear suddenly came crashing down on me. It was a big moment of victory. But it wasn't *my* victory.

It was the ghoul's victory.

Rain started to pour down. Everyone ran toward the parking lot. But I dropped to my knees on the grass and let the cold raindrops soak me.

I need help, I told myself.

I need to get rid of this ghoul. Get rid of Phears. Get rid of all the talk about that horrible Plover School.

Nicky? Tara? Where are you?

You promised to help me. And you didn't show.

I really need your help now. We need to help each other.

So where are you? Why didn't you keep your promise?

# 25

"**NICKY, WE HAVE TO** hurry," Tara said. "We promised Max we'd be at his game."

"I keep drifting in and out," I said, trying to shake myself awake. "It's like I take short naps or something." I pounded my fists together. "I *hate* being a ghost."

Tara stood in front of Max's dresser mirror. She leaned toward it and started to straighten the sleeves of her sweater. She sighed. "I hate it too, Nicky. I keep forgetting that I have no reflection. Every time I look into a mirror and don't see myself, I feel really sad."

Phears' cat let out a low sad whimper. It seemed to be right on the other side of the wall. But I knew it might be deep inside the mysterious tunnel.

"Poor Max," I said. "He's so scared of going back in that tunnel."

Tara turned to me, tugging at the floppy hat on her head. "I don't blame him. Who knows what kind of creatures are in that tunnel? I wish we could go with him. You know. Help him. But you remember what Lulu said. She said only living people can go in—and come back out."

I swallowed. "Once we have the cat, your plan will work, Tara. I know it will. Phears will be desperate to have his cat back. And he'll help us find Mom and Dad."

Tara shook her head. "It's our only chance. Mom's note just isn't helpful at all. And we don't have any other clues."

I pulled Tara away from the mirror. "Come on. Let's go find Max."

We started to the door—but stopped when we saw the little white mouse. It stood in the doorway on its back legs and sniffed the air with a twitching pink nose.

"Look, Nicky. Isn't he cute? He's so tiny."

"I don't think Max's parents would be too thrilled to know they have mice," I said.

Tara bent down to see the little guy better. "He looks like a cartoon mouse," she said. "Look at those little round button eyes."

She reached her hand down to pick it up—and the mouse *exploded*.

The blast made me cover my ears. It rocked the room— and pieces of mouse blew all over me. Frantically, I brushed mouse fur and guts off my shirt with both hands.

Thick smoke filled the bedroom. Tara and I started to choke.

"Nicky—what's happening?" Tara gasped.

I didn't have a chance to answer. The smoke swirled around a tall figure. Hidden in the haze, I recognized Phears! He looked exactly as Max had described him.

He raised his arms and his cloak slid around him like the swirling smoke. Lowering my eyes, I saw pieces of mouse fur and bones all over the carpet.

"This was easier than I thought," Phears boomed in a deep, vibrating voice. Each word made the black mist shiver.

I saw his hands reach out. Something slid from his fingers. It took me a moment to realize that his fingernails were stretching—sliding toward us, coiling around us like long snakes.

Tara let out a scream.

I opened my mouth to protest. Too late. The fingernails curled around our waists, taut as wire. Then they tightened, pulling us toward him, holding us prisoner.

"Too tight," I gasped. "Please—I can't breathe."

But the hard nails coiled tighter around my waist, cutting off my air. I couldn't move. I tried desperately to back away, to squirm free.

In the billowing black mist, Phears tossed back his head. And for a moment I saw his white eyes, solid white, no pupils at all. And I heard his soft laughter.

"Too easy," he whispered. "This was too easy, kids, wasn't it? I didn't even need my friend Max after all."

"Phears—" I choked out, struggling with both hands to loosen the sharp coils that stretched from his fingers. I turned and glimpsed Tara struggling too.

"Why do you want us?" I gasped. "What are you going to do to us?"

# 26

**THE LONG, SNAKELIKE FINGERNAILS** from Phears' left hand were wrapped tightly around Tara. The nails from his right hand circled me tightly, cutting through my clothes into my skin.

I tried backing up hard. Could I break the nails?

I twisted around and shot forward, leaning with all my weight. Then I dropped to my knees, trying to crack them. But no. The slender fingernails held as if made of steel.

"Stand still, Nicky," Phears boomed. "I'm in such a good mood because I've finally caught you. You don't want to spoil it for me, do you?"

The nails cut sharply into my waist. I turned to my sister. "Tara—we're ghosts. Why can't we disappear? Go invisible?"

"I . . . I've been trying," Tara whispered.

Phears snickered. "You won't escape that way. Try all you want. I'm holding you here."

"Well, what do you want?" I asked again. "Why have you been chasing us?"

"It's simple," Phears replied. And again I saw his glowing white eyes through the mist that covered his face. "I want you to take me to your parents."

"But we don't know where they are!" Tara cried.

"Liar!" Phears screamed. His snakelike fingernails lifted from Tara—then smacked her hard, like slender whips. *"Don't ever lie to me!"* Phears boomed.

"We . . . we're not lying," I stammered. "We thought *you* knew where they are."

"Liars! Liars!" Phears shouted. The five sharp fingernails slapped me hard. I staggered back, but the nails caught me, curled around me, and held me up.

The fog darkened around Phears. I could barely see him now. "It's so easy," he said softly. "Take me to your parents, and I'll let you go. I'll never bother you again."

Was he telling the truth?

It didn't matter. Tara and I didn't have a clue where our parents were.

"Take me to them," Phears repeated. "Take me there—now." And again the wiry nails pulled back like whips and slapped Tara and me hard.

"Please—stop!" Tara cried.

We're ghosts, I thought. Why does it hurt so much?

"Where are they hiding?" Phears growled. "I'm not going to wait much longer. Just tell me where your parents are hiding. Are they here? Here in this room?"

The nails tightened around my waist. "I . . . I can't breathe," I gasped.

I heard footsteps behind me. A cough. I turned to see Max step into the room.

"Hey, what's up?" he asked.

# 27

A FEW MINUTES EARLIER, I had no idea what was waiting for me in my room. I was hurrying home through the rain after the soccer match. I was drenched. My hair was soaked and raindrops poured down my face. But I didn't care. I needed to find Nicky and Tara and find out why they didn't keep their promise to show up.

I was angry and upset, and I could feel the Berserker Ghoul moving around inside me. I ran up the stairs in my wet soccer shoes, trailing mud on the carpet. My bedroom was dark, as if a black fog had settled inside. The fog should have been a warning, but I wasn't paying attention. I saw Nicky and Tara. I thought they were just standing there side by side.

I called, "Hey, what's up?"

And then I saw that they were tied up, with rope or something. And then I raised my eyes and squinted through the dark cloud—and saw Phears.

I finally caught on. This was why my two

ghost friends did not show at the soccer match. Phears had captured them.

"Welcome to the party, Max," Phears thundered. "You came just in time. We were about to leave to find their parents. Now you can join us."

"Uh, well . . . I'm kinda busy," I said, stalling for time.

Phears stared at me with his solid white eyes. My skin prickled. My hair stood straight up on end. "No jokes, Max. We've come to the end of the jokes. It's time to get serious. How have you enjoyed my Berserker friend? Have you and he become close?"

I didn't answer. I turned to Nicky and Tara. They were both struggling against the long cords wrapped around them. They seemed to be in a lot of pain. I followed the cords to Phears' hands, and I gasped when I saw that they were his fingernails.

Phears turned his stare on me again. And again my skin tingled and my hair stood straight up.

"Nicky and Tara are taking me to their parents," Phears said. "If they don't cooperate, they will disappear forever. And you, my friend Max . . . you . . ."

I felt a stab of fear run down my body. "Yes?" I asked, trembling.

"You will also disappear forever. You know too much. And you are of no use to me."

"Leave Max out of this!" Tara screamed.

"Too late," Phears said. "Too late for Max. Say goodbye to him now, kids. Max is history."

His eyes glowed brighter, like twin headlights through the fog. He turned them on me—and my skin started to burn. Wave after wave of heat rolled over me.

I couldn't turn away from the glowing eyes. Burning . . . burning me . . . as if my whole body was in flames.

"Goodbye, Max!" Phears shouted.

The last words I'd ever hear.

# 28

**"NO—WAIT!" I SCREAMED.**

My body thrashed and twisted and doubled over, collapsing in the heat of Phears' stare. My hair felt on fire. My arms and legs burned. My *tongue* burned.

*"Wait! Phears—I can be useful!"* I cried. *"I have something of yours that you want!"*

The fiery heat vanished as Phears turned his eyes away from me. I climbed back to my feet, my legs trembling.

"What do you have of mine, Max?" Phears demanded.

He held Nicky and Tara tightly in place. They both stared at me openmouthed, breathing hard.

"I . . . I have your cat!" I cried.

It was Phears' turn to let out a gasp of surprise. "You? You have Cha Cha?"

I nodded.

Would Tara's plan work? Would Phears make a deal with us for his cat?

If he didn't, we were doomed.

"Where is Cha Cha?" Phears demanded. His voice had changed. It was softer now. He couldn't hide how eager he was to see his cat. "Where is he? Are you lying, Max? It won't save your life."

"I have the cat," I lied. Was it still in the tunnel in the wall? I didn't hear it now. "But you'll have to make a trade."

"Trade?" he boomed. "Give me my cat, Max. Give Cha Cha to me now, or else—"

I took a deep breath. My whole body was shaking.

I wasn't making a trade with a kid on the playground. I was trying to make a deal with an evil ghost!

The words burst out of me: "I'll give you the cat if you let Nicky and Tara go. And if you remove the Berserker Ghoul from my body."

Phears glared at me. "Do you *dare* try to make a bargain with me?"

I stared back. "Let Nicky and Tara go," I repeated. "And get this ghoul out of me."

"And you'll give me my precious cat?" Phears said. "You'll give me back my Cha Cha?"

"That's the deal," I said, my heart thudding in my chest.

Would he go for it? Did he love his cat enough to make a deal?

He had to. He *had* to!

"Sorry. No deal," Phears said. "Say goodbye to your friends, Max."

He turned his white-eyed stare on me, and I felt a wave of heat sweep over my body. "Please— don't burn me! Don't burn me!" I cried.

# 29

**A CAT MEOWED.**

I had dropped to my knees with my head covered, trying to protect myself from the fiery heat. Suddenly, the burning stopped.

The cat meowed again.

"Cha Cha!" Phears cried. "It *is* you!"

I climbed slowly to my feet, my skin still burning.

"Bring him to me, Max!" Phears ordered. "Cha Cha! I'm coming! Can you hear me? Bring him to me right now, Max."

"And you'll let Nicky and Tara go? And send the Berserker Ghoul away?" I asked.

"Of course," Phears replied. "I promise. Cha Cha! Where are you?"

I turned to Nicky and Tara. They were still held prisoner, wrapped in the disgusting fingernails. Tara nodded and smiled at me. Nicky flashed me a thumbs-up.

That cat is going to save us after all, I thought. I moved to the wall and gripped the loose panel. I heard the cat meow on the other side. I tugged the panel.

It didn't budge.

"Cha Cha? Where are you?" Phears' voice thundered behind me. "What is taking so long?"

"The cat is right here," I said. I tightened my grip on the wall panel—and pulled.

Will the tunnel be here this time? It has to be! Please, please let it be there!

I gave another tug—and the panel slid off the wall. Yes! I could see the dark tunnel behind it. I felt a whoosh of cold air. It smelled so sour, I gagged.

With the wood panel in my hands, I staggered back to get away from the putrid smell. And as I backed up, a creature let out a wild shriek—and came flying out of the tunnel, sailing over my head.

I spun around—and saw the black cat. A ghost cat—I could see right through it. It leaped onto Phears' arm. "Cha Cha! Cha Cha!" Phears cried happily. "You're back!"

The black cat snuggled its head against Phears' cheek and purred softly. "Cha Cha, I've missed you *so* much," Phears declared.

"Now let us go," Tara cried, tugging at the coiled fingernails around her waist.

"Yes. Hurry, Phears," I said. "You've got your cat. Now keep your promise. Get rid of the Berserker Ghoul, too."

127

The cat was tucked under his chin. Phears turned to me. "Here's the lesson of the day, Max," he said. "You should never trust an evil old ghost. I've got my cat. And I've got my two prisoners. I guess I have everything I need—and you have nothing. Thanks for the cat, Max. Now say good-bye to your friends. So sorry to see you go."

*"No!"* I screamed. "You can't *do* that! That's *not* fair!"

Furious, I raised the wood panel above my head—and heaved it at Phears.

It sailed right through him. But the cat let out a startled shriek—and leaped from Phears' neck onto me! It dug its claws into my shoulder and let out another shrill shriek in my ear, holding on tight.

Phears' fingernails curled away from Nicky and Tara. The nails quickly slid back into his fingers. He came toward me, reaching out with both hands. "Give me that cat!"

I felt a tremor of fear inside me. Felt the Berserker Ghoul move—fast. The ghoul was afraid of the cat. I could feel its fear!

My right ear suddenly throbbed with pain. I grabbed it and felt a powerful whoosh of hot wind. Yellow smoke poured from my ear.

No. Not smoke. The ghoul. Frightened by the cat, the Berserker Ghoul poured out of my body in a funnel cloud of yellow smoke.

Phears grabbed the cat off my shoulder. "Give it back! Come back, Cha Cha!"

As he held the cat to his chest, I saw the yellow smoke rise above him—then dive. Yes! The ghoul poured quickly into Phears' ear! The yellow smoke swirled down into Phears' ear until it disappeared completely.

Holding on to the black cat, Phears turned to Nicky and Tara. "Jabba gubbba!" he bellowed. Then he did a wild cartwheel into the wall.

"Hubbba gubbbba!" Phears screamed. He began to spin crazily. Then he turned another cartwheel. "Gubbba gubbbbba?"

His eyes were no longer white. They had a yellow glow, bright as the sun. He bounced off the walls, jabbering nonsense words. Then he jumped out the window and went running down the street, turning somersaults, the cat clinging to his back.

"Yes—!" A major victory. Without the ghoul inside, I felt so light, so free, so . . . *me*!

"We're free!" Nicky cried. "He's gone!"

Tara shook herself hard as if she didn't believe it. "Thank you, Brainimon!" she shouted.

Nicky, Tara, and I slapped high fives all around. We shouted for joy. We couldn't stop laughing. Phears looked like such a jerk, possessed by that insane ghoul!

Was he gone for good?

I didn't want to think about that. I just wanted to celebrate being normal again.

But the celebration was cut short when Dad suddenly came striding into the room. Nicky and Tara vanished.

I took a deep breath and tried to act calm and nonchalant. "Hey, Dad, what's up?"

"Good news," he said, grinning. "You have an interview at the Plover School first thing tomorrow morning!"

# 30

Dear Diary,

The Plover School looks more like a prison than a school. It has dark green walls and low ceilings—and some of the windows even have bars on them. I didn't hear any laughing or shouting or loud voices. I think it's because the kids have to wear gray uniforms all day, and that puts them in a dreary mood. (And the uniforms probably itch really bad too.)

I was interviewed by a man named Captain Randall. He explained that the Plover School isn't a military school. But everyone has a rank, and you have to call everyone by their rank.

Captain Randall is pretty old. I mean, he has white hair and a lot of wrinkles in his forehead. But he sat up very straight, like a soldier, and he kinda barked his questions at me.

I was a little scared before we started to talk. But once the interview started, I thought it went very well.

First, Captain Randall asked me how I liked school.

I said, "Jabbba jabbba gubbba."

He narrowed his tiny, steel-colored eyes at me. "I didn't really hear you. Tell me, Max, what are you interested in? What are your favorite subjects?"

"Hubbba gubbba?" I replied. And then I dropped to the floor and started to roll around the room.

Captain Randall jumped to his feet. "Max, what's wrong?" he cried.

"Hubbbba jabbbba," I said. I climbed up, lowered my head, and went crashing into the chalkboard. I hit it so hard, it cracked in two. Then I went spinning crazily around the room four or five times, knocking over chairs, tables, everything in sight.

And that pretty much ended the interview.

When I got back home, I told Nicky and
Tara all about it. They both looked confused.

"So you were rejected by the Plover
School?" Nicky asked.

I nodded. "Yeah. Do you believe it? They
told Dad never to bring me there again. Is
that cool or what?"

Tara tugged at one of her earrings.
"But Max, the Berserker Ghoul flew out of
your body yesterday. We saw it go."

"Yeah, I know," I replied.

"So . . . you mean _another_ ghoul possessed your body?" Nicky asked.

"No. No other ghoul," I said.

Then I burst out laughing. And they did too. They finally caught on to what I had done.

Hey, they don't call me Brainimon for nothing.

Of course, I can't keep this page in my diary. I don't want Ms. McDonald to see it. She'd never believe any of it. She'd accuse me of writing fiction and give me a big fat F.

So I'm ripping out this page too. So far, I've ripped out almost all the pages in this journal.

Will Phears return and bring more of

his ghostly friends? Will Nicky and Tara find their parents? And will they find out what turned them into ghosts?

Sorry, Diary. I can't write about any of that. If I did, I'd have to tear out those pages too.

Maybe I'll write about how it rained today. It was a pretty good rain. I can describe the clouds and the puddles and everything. Ms. McDonald will really like that. . . .

## TO BE CONTINUED

## ABOUT THE AUTHOR

**Robert Lawrence Stine's** scary stories have made him one of the bestselling children's authors in history. "Kids like to be scared!" he says, and he has proven it by selling more than 300 million books. R.L. teamed up with Parachute Press to create Fear Street, the first and number one bestselling young adult horror series. He then went on to launch Goosebumps, the creepy bestselling series that gave kids chills all over the world and made him the number one children's author of all time (*The Guinness Book of Records*).

R.L. Stine lives in Manhattan with his wife, Jane, their son, Matthew, and their dog, Nadine. He says he has never seen a ghost—but he's still looking!